CEDAR
DANCE

CEDAR DANCE

A NOVEL

MONICA NAWROCKI

yellow dog

Yellow Dog
(an imprint of Great Plains Publications)
1173 Wolseley Avenue
Winnipeg, MB R3G 1H1
www.greatplains.mb.ca

Great Plains Publications gratefully acknowledges the financial
support provided for its publishing program by the Government of
Canada through the Canada Book Fund; the Canada Council for the
Arts; the Province of Manitoba through the Book Publishing Tax
Credit and the Book Publisher Marketing Assistance Program; and
the Manitoba Arts Council.

Design & Typography by Relish New Brand Experience
Printed in Canada by Friesens

Library and Archives Canada Cataloguing in Publication

Title: Cedar dance / Monica Nawrocki.
Names: Nawrocki, Monica, 1965- author.
Identifiers: Canadiana (print) 2019005624X | Canadiana
    (ebook) 20190056258 | ISBN 9781773370163 (softcover) |
    ISBN 9781773370170 (EPUB) | ISBN 9781773370187 (Kindle)
Classification: LCC PS8627.A97 C43 2019 | DDC jC813/.6—dc23

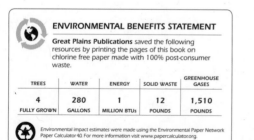

*To my mom, Faith Wyse, who first introduced
me to the wonderful world of words*

CHAPTER 1

You know how sometimes you'll be watching a movie and something unbelievable will happen, and you just want to yell, *AS IF!*?

Well, this story has a few of those, but I swear everything in it is the truth. I'll get the first one out of the way right now: my mom and I were born on the same day.

I was a scrawny baby boy who arrived on her eighteenth birthday. She had planned to spend that day having her name legally changed from Carol Bronski to Moon Dance, but I changed her plans. Well, actually I only delayed them. Unfortunately.

Now she's a thirty-year-old Moon Dance. (That makes me twelve, for those of you reading this during summer vacation and refusing to do math.) Personally, I have always felt Mom looked more like a Carol Bronski than a Moon Dance. She's fairly tall and would be considered athletic, I think, if she did anything athletic. Is marching in protests a sport yet?

My mom ran away from home a couple of months after her seventeenth birthday to join an anti-logging protest called Camp Douglas. In the span of just a few weeks, she fell in and out of love with a man named

Shell and got pregnant. She didn't find out I was on the way until after Shell had moved on to a bigger protest.

Mom went back home to Grandma and Grandpa. A bad day for everyone, I would imagine. The Grands supported her until I was three. Mom went to secretarial school while the Grands took care of me and then she joined a temp agency. That means when a regular office worker has to miss work, the company will call the temp agency to send someone like my mom to take their place, *temp*orarily.

If you ask Mom what she does for a living, she'll tell you she's a spy for Mother Earth – so do me a favour and don't ask. She snoops. She works in different offices all over the city and as soon as she gets a chance, she checks into the company's environmental policies – the real ones, not the ones they publicize. Then she writes about them on her blog, created with a secret identity which I have promised never to reveal, so don't ask about that either.

Anyway, when I was three, we moved out of the Grands' place and into our own apartment, which I hate. We almost got a two-bedroom apartment when I was five, but the Grands gave Mom a choice between help with rent for a bigger place or tuition for me to go to private school and she chose the Crazy Hippie School of Peace and Love and Other Crap, also known as the Community Harmony School. More about that later.

Our apartment is so small, Mom sleeps on a pull-out sofa bed and keeps her clothes in the front closet with our coats and boots, which is where my story starts: I was in the closet, rummaging for a duffel bag to take on our class trip to camp, when Mom came home from work with a brand-new used suitcase from her favourite thrift store.

"No," I said as soon as I saw the suitcase.

"Hello, Cedar," she said. "How was your day? Mine was fine, thanks, except for the part where I walked an extra ten blocks to get my son a new suitcase to take to camp." She kicked off her sandals and dropped the weaved basket she carries instead of a normal-mother purse.

"No," I said. "And my name is Charles."

I have recently resumed my campaign to be called by my first name in my own home. Doesn't that sound like a basic human right to you? My name is Charles (same as my Grandpa), my middle name is Cedar (because Mom's a tree-hugger), my last name is Dance (I don't want to talk about it). Mom calls me Cedar, my school friends call me Chuck (or worse), my grandpa calls me Charles, and my Grandma manages to never use a name at all. She doesn't like to take sides.

I pulled the green duffel bag out from the tangle of junk on the floor of the closet and held it up to her. "I'm using this." Grandpa and I had found it last May at the army surplus store. It still smelled like mosquito repellent. Last year's camp was a bug fest.

"Sweetie, you're in sixth grade now. Don't you think a suitcase would be more appropriate for your last year of camp?"

My last year of camp also meant my last year at Community Harmony School and I was a tad freaked out about that. CHS is small – only fifty kids in the whole school. Next year, I'll be going to a big junior high, and after all this time with the granola crowd, I'm nervous about the new school. My best friend, Jessica, says junior high will be a breath of fresh air after the claustrophobia of the same small group of kids for six years. She lives in a different part of the city so we'll be going to different schools. She'll never pass math without me.

Jessica is the one who renamed CHS the "City Hippie School." The first time she used the word *hippie*, I asked her what she meant. Her mouth literally dropped open.

"How can you live with a hippie and not know what a hippie is?" she asked me.

"You think my mom is a hippie?"

Jessica rolled her eyes. "First of all, your mom cooks everything from scratch, she makes her own clothes, cuts her own hair, drinks carrot juice, shops at thrift stores, won't buy anything she can't recycle, doesn't own a TV or a car or a computer or even a cell phone, and would probably live in the woods in a converted school bus if she could make it work."

I nodded. "All true. Anything else?"

"Yes!" she almost yelled. "You are here because of her 'summer of love!' That's such a hippie thing!"

"Oh. I thought that hippies only lived in the '60s," I said.

"Chuck, seriously? Your mom *is* living in the '60s."

I took the duffel bag back to my room and started throwing clothes in.

"Cedar, slow down and let me help. Are you sure you want that shirt? It makes you look so ... thin."

I gave Mom the glare. She meant scrawny. I *am* scrawny; every single person in my class is taller, wider, and heavier than me. And that includes the fifth-graders! (We have two grades in every class in my school.) Smaller than the fifth-graders. Now that's embarrassing.

I assume my father was scrawny. And had brown hair and eyes. And poor eyesight. Everyone in my family is built like a refrigerator, has blond hair and blue eyes, and can spot a four-leaf clover from a half-mile away. In my mom's case, this may be partly due to the gallons of carrot juice she drinks. I wear glasses that are too big for my scrawny face. My mom believes in buying everything several sizes too big for me to grow into.

I clamped my front teeth together. "I like this shirt," I said. I've recently perfected gritted-teeth-talking.

"Oh, honey. What about this one? It's so perfect for camp."

I gasped. It was tie-dyed. "Are you serious?"

Mom folded the t-shirt and put it in the bag. "Your stuff would stay nice and flat in the suitcase. I know you like your things folded, Cedar." She brushed strands of blond hair away from her eyes. There was always a haze of hair in her face, escapees from the long, single braid she constructed every morning.

"I don't like my things folded, in case you didn't notice. And my name is Charles." I grabbed the tie-dyed t-shirt out of the bag, tossed it into the closet, and then made a point of ruffling two shirts unnecessarily before ramming them to the bottom of the bag.

"Fine," she sighed. "I'll get your beach towel. I think I know where it is." She left and I quickly pulled the clothes out of the duffel bag, folded them, and put them back in. I threw in my flashlight, bug spray, sunscreen, and plastic food wrap. You heard me, food wrap – Jessica and I had practical joke plans.

"You need underwear for two weeks. Do you have enough?" she yelled from the kitchen. If I didn't answer, Mr. Staff from the apartment next door might. Not much soundproofing in our building.

Speaking of Mr. Staff, here's a story that will tell you about the kind of person Mom is. I don't want you to get the wrong impression just because *I* find her annoying.

Last year, when Mr. Staff moved in, he was horrible to my mom and me. He came over to complain about Mom hanging towels on our balcony railing and about the noise. He complained if Mom left her umbrella out in the hallway to dry or if my boots were one inch off the mat outside our door.

He scowled at me when I said hello and one day he said, "Keep your hello to yourself, you little brat. And get a haircut."

That was it for me – he'd been rude to me many times when Mom wasn't around and I always kept it to myself. But I told her about the "brat" comment and she said, "Okay. Enough is enough." She never says stuff like that, so I was excited to see what she would do.

She made cookies.

"Mom! What are you going to do about Mr. Staff?" I asked.

"I'm doing it," she replied. "You want to help?"

"Okay. Are we going to put laxatives in them?" I asked.

Mom stopped and stared at me. "What a thing to say! I hope you're joking." She resumed mixing. "We're going to get to know him. Starting with taking him a batch of cookies. Who can stay cranky with a plate of warm cookies in their hands?"

"Are you kidding me? He insults me all the time and you reward him with cookies? I can't believe this!"

Mom put down the wooden spoon. "Cedar, is that actually how you see this?"

"Is there another way to see it?" I sputtered, my face flushing with anger.

She studied me for a moment. "You know, one of the best things your grandpa taught me was to choose to believe the best about people. That would be an excellent 'thought for the day,'" she said. (I'll explain *that* later.)

"That does *not* sound like Grandpa," I said.

"Well, his wording was a little different, but the idea was the same."

"What was his wording?"

"He used to say, 'if you can't decide if someone is evil or stupid, choose stupid; it's easier to live with.'"

"*That* sounds like Grandpa," I said. "But it's not the same thing at all."

"Sure, it is. He's saying that what we choose to believe about others only affects us, not them. So, you may as well choose to believe something that is easier on you."

She smiled at me and I scowled back. "So, where do the cookies fit into your weird little theory?" I asked her.

"We let Mr. Staff know we want to be friends. Maybe one day, we'll find out where all that anger comes from."

I had nothing to say to that. I helped make the cookies. I even went with her when she delivered them. In the interest of science.

I watched closely as she handed Mr. Staff the plate of warm cookies. It was quick, but I saw a strange little twist of his mouth. And I can report, for science, that a year later, Mom and Mr. Staff often have tea and he never yells at us anymore or complains. In fact, he even grunts back when I say hello.

Anyhow, every once in a while, if one of us yells a question to the other in this apartment with paper-thin walls, Mr. Staff answers. It's as close as Mr. Staff ever comes to joking, but I didn't want to hear him yelling about my underwear.

"Will you please keep it down?" I yelled back to Mom.

I dug my bathing suit out of a drawer and was shoving it into the bag when the phone rang. I could hear Mom talking to Grandpa. Hopefully he was calling to offer me a ride to school in the morning. We don't have a car and taking the city bus with this big bag was not my idea of a good time.

"Cedar, Grandpa wants to talk to you."

It's Charles, I silent-screamed so hard I almost burst a blood vessel in my forehead. Seriously, I felt it bulge a little.

"Hey, Grandpa."

"Hello, Charles," boomed Grandpa. "So, she hasn't killed you yet, then?"

"Not yet," I said. Grandpa says this every single time he calls our house. It bugs Mom. That's probably why I still think it's funny after the 86-millionth time. "How's Grandma?" I asked.

"Like a headless chicken," he said.

"Hello, lovey," Grandma yelled.

She mumbled something else in the background and Grandpa said, "Did you get that, boy?"

"No."

"She wants to know how you did on the test."

"Which one?" I asked. I'd been whining about a couple recently.

"Which one?" he shouted.

Mumble, mumble.

"Did you get that, boy?"

"No."

"She says the science test."

"Oh. I got eighty-four percent."

"Eighty-four," he shouted. I pulled the phone away from my ear just in time. Every phone conversation I'd ever had with my Gran has been through someone else. She refuses to get on the phone. Says talking on the phone makes her feel like an astronaut. I have no idea what that means.

"How about I drive you to school tomorrow?" said Grandpa. "What time does the bus leave for camp?"

"Eight o'clock sharp. What time should I be ready?"

"I'll be there at seven and we'll stop for hot chocolate and a doughnut on the way. Last chance for good food for two weeks. Hang on a sec." I pulled the phone back a few inches. "What?" he bellowed at Grandma, then spoke to me again. "She wants to know if you packed some candy to take to Camp Nutritious."

This was another of Grandpa's ongoing jokes. I delivered my line: "Where would I get candy here in the House of Fibre Goodness?"

Grandpa laughed.

"Yeah, he said it," he shouted to Grandma.

CHAPTER 2

I think when they design school buses, they do something special to the wall panels so that noise echoes back and forth, getting louder with every bounce. I had a headache by the time we hit the outer limits of the city. A busload of grade five and six kids freed from the concrete jungle into the wild is a bit like what you'd get if you opened all the cages at the zoo during a full moon. Even if "the wild" is just a tidy camp a few miles out of the city.

With the bus bouncing up and down on its non-existent shock absorbers, it was hard to focus on Jessica's face, but I was pretty sure she looked exasperated.

"What?" I demanded, as I untangled a knot in my hair.

"Seriously, Chuck, what is the deal with you and your hair? You have gone to the barber every three months for the past two years and you still haven't cut it. Then you whine about how you hate your long hair. What's the problem?" Jessica's own brown hair was shoulder length, only slightly shorter than mine. Hers was usually in a ponytail and was not her top priority in life.

"It's Charles, and I told you – the problem is my mom." I could feel my face getting hot. "She loves my

long hair," I whispered. "You know – the Shell thing."
I looked around to make sure no one was listening,
although it was doubtful anyone could hear over the
roar of the asthmatic bus engine.

"What shell thing? You mean the Donor?"

"Please don't call him that. Yes, I mean my father,
Shell. My hair is just like his, apparently, and Mom has
this thing about it."

Mom's usually quite practical about Shell. She never
says their "encounter" was stupid – probably because
she thinks that would make me feel like I was a mistake,
which I obviously was – but she never gets all sentimen-
tal about it. My hair is the only thing she's ever weird
about, so it makes it impossible for me to wreck it for
her. I wonder how much she thinks about him. I always
pretend I'm not interested and that I never think about
him. But I do. A lot. Not the real him, of course, because
I don't know the first thing about him. But my Fantasy
Dad is amazing. Superman and Santa Claus combined
into one perfect human being whose only concern in
the world is my happiness. You get the picture.

"What does your mom say when you keep coming
back from the barber without a haircut?" Jessica asked.

"I never tell her I'm going."

"What? How do you get her to give you the money?"
Jessica rummaged through her backpack while she talked.

"I tell her we're fundraising to save a tree or a whale
or something."

Some people steal for candy. I lie for haircuts. And
this is how it goes every time: I go to the barber shop,

I sit in the chair, I tell him to take it off, he asks if I'm sure, I picture my mom's face if I came home with short hair. Then, I get out of the chair, I go to the bank, and I deposit the money into the account my mom helped me open to save for a bike. (When we say "bike," she visualizes an environmentally friendly bicycle and I see a loud, smelly motorbike. So it's not actually a lie, is it?)

I'll bet you're thinking that I have a thing for Jessica, but I don't. She's more like a sister. We've just always been friends. Every once in a while, one of the idiots at school decides to tease us but not too often anymore.

The first time it happened, I was by myself and I sputtered and muttered and hurried away with a red face. The second time it happened, Jessica and I were eating lunch together and one of the older boys made some comment about me being the best she could do for a boyfriend and she gave him the verbal beating of his life. Now, if anyone gives me a hard time, I use one of Jessica's lines on them. But if we're together when it happens, I just sit back and enjoy the show.

Jessica found what she was looking for in her backpack and sat up straight. "Well, you better decide before September. Get it cut or be proud of it, but either way, you better not be all anxious about it. Junior high kids can smell fear. Like hyenas." She strained to see the front of the bus.

"What are you doing?" I asked.

"I'm trying to see if Melvin can see me in the Spy Cam. I'm starving."

I looked up at the giant rear-view mirror above the bus driver's head. Melvin looked uncharacteristically focussed on the road at the moment.

"Looks busy – go for it. And give me some."

We scrunched down in the seat and ate homemade oatmeal raisin cookies. Jessica's three older brothers all like raisins in their oatmeal cookies, but Jessica doesn't. She treats the raisins in her cookies the same way she treats the seeds in her watermelon – whether she's inside or outside. She shot one out of the corner of her mouth and hit Pacific in the back of the head.

"I saw that!" Melvin shouted. We hunkered down even further.

The bus slowed and ground to a halt. I wondered what the penalty for raisin-spewing was, but Jessica was not the reason he'd stopped.

"Check it out. A protest," said Pacific, pointing at a crowd of people filling the road in front of the bus.

I popped back up to see what was happening. There were about twenty-five or thirty people blocking the road. Some had signs, some were walking, and some were sitting around in little groups talking, drinking from thermoses, and eating cookies. Apparently without raisins since no one was spitting.

"Why don't we just walk the rest of the way?" Jessica said. "The driveway to the camp is right up there. I can see it."

"They can't let anyone through. That's the point of a blockade," Pacific said.

"That's stupid, and who died and made you the king

of blockades, Pacific?" demanded Mouth, so-named for obvious reasons.

"I've been to millions of these things with my parents," Pacific said. "I was practically born and raised at protest marches."

The bus door wheezed open and someone stepped on. We all strained to see. Melvin and the teachers were having a little whisper-conference at the front of the bus with one of the protestors who had an itchy-looking beard that said, *I've been camping for weeks.* The adults seemed to come to some sort of agreement, and Mr. Grubby-face got off the bus. The PE teacher, Mr. George (the only non-hippie member of our school staff), announced that we would be walking the rest of the way to camp and that Melvin would circle back and take the alternate route with the bus and our luggage. He sounded a little disgusted, but Miss Blanchard, our classroom teacher, clapped her palms together in gleeful anticipation of this unplanned field trip into the wonderful world of peaceful protest.

As we filed off the bus, the protesters all stood up and greeted us as though they hadn't seen any outsider humans for days. There were all kinds of people there, all shapes and sizes and colours and ages and styles. It surprised me. I always pictured these camps as being full of Shells and Moons, teenagers with big ideas. But you couldn't say that about this crowd. And they seemed organized too. I could see tents in the trees – it looked like a big camp.

Miss Blanchard was clapping her hands like a seal. "Gather. Gather, people."

She waved us all toward her and we shuffled into a messy semi-circle around her.

"Now, why did we bring you to camp? Anyone?" Miss Blanchard was barely able to conceal her excitement. Jessica and I exchanged glances.

"For s'mores, obviously," Jessica whispered.

"Obviously," I whispered back.

"No one?" asked Miss Blanchard. "We brought you to camp to learn, people. To learn. And we have just been gifted with a lovely opportunity to learn about the anti-logging movement. This man is called Fungus. He will answer any questions you have about the anti-logging movement. Who has a question?"

And that's when the zomb-bomb dropped. Sometimes, kids just have an instinct for when to zombie-out. We wanted to get to Camp Mingle and, you know, mingle!

Mouths dropped open slightly and eyes lost focus, staring blindly into the distance. Shoulders sagged, making arms look orangutan-long.

"No one has a question?" Miss Blanchard sounded appalled.

Someone muttered "which way to the beach?" from the safety of the crowd.

Everyone tittered and Miss Blanchard's expression changed in a way that suggested we would be settling in here to do some "quality learning."

"All right then, I will ask the questions, shall I?" I thought she was going to ask Fungus some questions on our behalf. For the learning. But instead of turning towards the hippie with the answers, she turned to us.

"Now then, what kind of forest are we standing in?" She pursed her lips and ran her gaze across a sea of vacant expressions.

When it became evident that we wouldn't be able to zombie out of our lesson, someone at the back said, "Temperate rainforest."

Jessica and I looked at each other and rolled our eyes. Brian. Why are guys named Brian always so smart? Must be because of the name. Brian is awfully close to Brain.

"And what kind of trees are we looking at here?" Miss Blanchard asked happily.

"Fir," cooed Brian the Brain.

"And what else?" Miss Blanchard's face escaped into a huge, goofy grin. Her I'm-about- to-make-a-joke face looked a lot like Mr. George's I'm-about-to-fart face.

I glanced around at all the cedar trees and my heart sank. She was staring at me.

"Hmm?" she hummed. "What kind of trees are these?" She swept her hand toward the nearest clump of trees like she was announcing a studio full of cash and prizes, then zeroed in on me with her eyebrows raised in anticipation.

I pressed my lips together and stared at my shoes.

She turned to Fungus who was watching all of this with a rather concerned expression on his face. You could almost hear him thinking, *If the future is in the hands of these morons, we're in trouble!*

"You see Mr. Fungus, we actually have a student named Cedar! Isn't that wonderful?"

"Cool. And it's just Fungus. No 'Mr.'"

Miss Blanchard returned her beam to me. "So, Cedar, what kind of trees are these?"

"It's *Charles*, and those are truffula trees," I muttered at the ground. Jessica snorted trying to swallow a giggle. There was laughter amongst the kids closest to me who heard my answer.

"Sorry, *Ce-dar*," Miss Blanchard over-enunciated. "Can you repeat that a little louder please?"

"Truffala," I shouted and the whole class burst out laughing.

Miss Blanchard turned the colour of The Lorax as Fungus shuffled away. She was about to stop him, but Pacific had everyone in stitches because he was insisting truffala trees were real. I thought Brian's head was going to explode. The ensuing chaos defeated Miss Blanchard, as it often does, and she sighed and started walking up the road toward Camp Mingle.

All the zombies turned back into excited campers as we followed our disappointed teacher up the road.

"You know she's gonna make us come back and have a lesson with that guy. We should have just gotten it over with," I said to Jessica as we trudged along in the middle of the group.

Jessica shrugged. "How many times can you have the same lesson? Forest good. Loggers bad."

"Well, I wouldn't go that far," I said. "Forest good. Clear-cutting bad. Greedy companies bad. Loggers have to eat too."

Pacific, who was directly in front of us, turned around and walked backwards. "Chuckie Cheese, if there were no loggers willing to do the work, the forests would be safe."

"Excellent idea, Pacific. We'll fire every logger in the country, save the forest, and start writing our school assignments in the dirt," I said.

"And wiping our butts with leaves. Is it okay to use the leaves, Pacific?" Kevin asked, bouncing into the conversation.

Pacific fake-laughed at Kevin. "Don't be stupid. There are alternatives to all the paper products we use, you know. Like bamboo, for one."

"Excellent idea," said Jessica. "We'll just move the clear-cutting operation a bit south and carry on!" Brian appeared suddenly, crashing into me in his hurry to join the conversation.

"Oops, sorry, Chuck. The issue is not logging vs not logging, you guys. It's clear-cutting vs sustainable forestry practices. And most of those are win-win. For example, increasing the time between harvests actually creates higher quality timber, in addition to protecting the ecosystem. If you select the trees you take, the habitats can be maintained or easily re-established. In fact, just the other day I was reading…"

"Brian!" Jessica and I shouted at the same time.

He blinked at us. "What?"

"Give us a break," I said. "We all know this stuff. Protect the marshland, protect old-growth, put limits around rivers and creeks, protect spawning grounds, blah, blah, blah."

This was normal conversation at my house. Conservation conversation.

Brian/Brain was still blinking at me.

"My point is, Brian, that *we* know this stuff. And while we are the ones who would really like to still have a forest and an ice cap and a global temperature we can survive, *we* are not at the controls. Yet. Get back to me when you're the CEO of a multi-national logging corporation and then we'll talk."

Brian frowned, blinked again, and slithered back into the glob of kids, muttering about community forests.

Now Jessica was gaping at me. "What was that all about?" she asked.

I shrugged. How do you explain doomed-planet stress to someone who believes harsher fines for littering will save the world? I heard way too much information from my mom about the state of the environment and our bleak future. And it stressed me out.

We were almost at the turn-off to Camp Mingle when Pacific called my name. I turned to look at him and he pointed at one of the protestors. A thin, short man carried an armful of wood through our line to get to the camp on the other side of the road. "Maybe you weren't hatched after all, Chuckie Cheese. I think I just found your daddy." Pacific laughed loudly and kept walking.

The man carrying the wood turned his head then and both Jessica and I got a good look at his face at the same moment.

"Holy cow," Jessica said.

Put some glasses on this guy and he was me.

CHAPTER 3

By noon, we had settled into our cabins. I got a bottom bunk and David was on the one above me. I liked all the guys in my cabin. Mr. George was our cabin leader and he was okay. You just had to get used to him. More bark than bite, as Mom would say.

As I was laying out my sleeping bag and making sure my bed was tidy, I realized every other guy in my cabin had just thrown his stuff onto his bunk. The boys were all gathered around the little woodstove we weren't allowed to use, goofing around and telling jokes. I quickly bunched up my sleeping bag into a messy heap.

Thought for the day: Fit in!

I wasn't a total outcast at my school, but I did tend to live at the edges of the action, if you know what I mean. I hung around the periphery of whatever was going on until I was absorbed into it. Especially if Jessica wasn't around. I never started any of the fun. Hardly ever contributed any ideas either. But in this small group of six boys, it might be easier to step up and be one of the gang.

I guess I should explain the "thought for the day." My mom is a big believer in something she calls "living with intention." It is far too hippie-woo-woo to get into, but the one thing I like is how she chooses a thought for the day. Hers are things like this: *Be true to yourself.*

Mine are more practical: *Don't let Stefano get to you.* (Stefano is a fifth-grader in my class who really drives me nuts.) *Do one thing today that scares you. Be kind to Mr. Staff even if he's in a bad mood. Don't mouth-off to Mom.*

I don't do this every day, just when I have a problem or something happens, like noticing that I am already on the outskirts of my cabin social circle on the first day. So, I make up a thought for the day. Like a goal, that's all. *Fit in!*

When I first started making up TFTDs, I was kind of into it and I shared it with Jessica. No one else! In her usual enthusiastic way, she thought it was a great idea and said she was going to do it every day. That lasted three days. But she still does it occasionally. Hers are usually lines from movies. Bad ones. And the theme is usually revenge. This is yet another Jessica quirk that I have attributed to her having three older brothers. I think she may actually have a payback list that she is slowly working through, one brother at a time. She calls them SAVs. That stands for Secret Acts of Vengeance. I hope I never get on her bad side.

So, as if it isn't crazy enough just having four teen-agers living in the same house, they always seem to be at war. Either a prank, a prank response, vengeance for the prank response, revenge for the vengeance, revenge for the revenge … Jessica's house is a three-ring circus of secret missions and double agents.

I love visiting, but I wouldn't want to live there. When the chaos gets to be too much, I just sneak off home to my carrot juice-swilling, Enya-playing, incense-burning mother and help her make solstice decorations out of lemongrass. DO NOT tell anyone I admitted that.

Anyhow, I joined my cabinmates around the stove and it was fun. I even told a joke.

There was another school at camp, same as last year, but we bunked with kids from our own school. When they put us into activity groups, they mixed us up with the St. Joe's kids.

St. Joseph's was a private school too, but it was Catholic. Not a hippie in sight. Their class was a five-six split like ours, so our sixth-graders knew theirs from last year.

When the whole camp met in the dining hall for the usual introductions and rules and all that, I scanned the St. Joe's crowd for familiar faces. I spotted Jessica with her cabin group, making faces at me to try to make me laugh.

When they called out our names for the activity groups, Jessica and I were together. Our group's first activity was a hike, so we were all dismissed from the dining hall that smelled like tomato soup and told to go get what we needed from our cabins.

We met at the fire circle, hanging around on the benches that surround the firepit waiting for everyone to get there. Eventually, we set off with two leaders who looked like they'd lost the coin toss for activities. Their boredom was contagious. I wondered why the leaders weren't talking about the forest and stuff. Wasn't that the point of a nature hike? The trees we were trudging past were enormous. I may be a city boy, but my mom made sure I could tell the difference between a Douglas fir and a cedar. I liked the trail we were on – it was narrow but clear. Obviously well-worn. I especially liked the shiny leaves of the salal bushes that pushed into the trail on either side. Salal was the perfect groundcover for forest – it never grew much higher than your waist so you could see over it. Even *I* could see over it.

Before long, Jessica and I were lagging further and further behind the group, discussing our evil plan. She had smuggled in some plastic wrap too.

"Hey, look." Jessica came to a standstill and pointed off into the bush to our right.

"What?" I asked, squinting in the direction of her finger.

"What is that big lump there, the one between those two trees? Do you see it?"

I jammed my glasses into the bridge of my nose and squinted harder. "It looks like a big rock with moss on it. So?"

"It's a weird shape. Let's go check it out."

We veered off the trail and crashed through bushes and stepped over fallen trees. The closer we got, the weirder the rock looked.

"It's an old car!" Jessica said.

It was so old, it appeared to be sinking right into the earth. The moss was a green monster inching its giant mouth around the car like a python devouring a cow. The tires were gone and the doors seemed to be growing out of the forest floor. There wasn't any glass left in the windows, but the roof was still all there. I poked my head through one of the windows and jumped back so fast I banged my head on the frame.

"What?" Jessica asked. She shoved her head through the same window but left hers inside.

I grabbed the tail of her shirt and pulled her backwards so I could take another look. What had surprised me was that someone appeared to be living in the car. There was a frying pan and a small pot, two big glass jars of water, a stuffed garbage bag with a blanket spilling out the top. Hanging neatly side by side on a branch wedged through the window frame were a black hoodie and a big, green raincoat.

"Let's get inside," Jessica said.

"Nope. Not me. I'm outta here," I said and started walking away, hoping Jessica would follow.

She did and we hurried back to the path. The rest of the group was way ahead of us now and well out of earshot. "Did you think that guy this morning looked like me?" I asked her.

"What guy?" Jessica has the attention span of a fruit fly.

"The protest guy. The one carrying the wood."

"Oh yeah! He *did* look like you. That was so weird. And it's funny that your dad was a protest guy..." She stopped walking and turned to look at me. "Jeez, Chuck, you think Pacific could be right? You think that guy might actually be your dad?"

My heart was pounding like you wouldn't believe. I had been thinking about that exact thing since I saw him, but hearing Jessica say it out loud made it seem possible. "I don't know. Do you think he could be?"

She frowned. "Well, he did look like you. And he seemed about the right age. And this is the area where your mom met him, right?" She looked at me and I nodded.

"It's possible," she said.

We were both quiet for a while, walking slowly and getting even further behind our group. The trail wound through the trees and I hadn't been able to see the others for a while. Now, even the sound of their voices was all but gone. I doubted we were missing anything.

Finally, Jessica spoke. "Well, if it was me, I'd wanna find out, one way or the other. We need a plan, Chuck."

"It's Charles, Jessica."

"It's Jess, Charles." She made an okay sign with her fingers, then reached out quickly and snicked the tip of my nose, snapping my head back and making my eyes water. I yelled and chased her down the path.

First thing after lunch (which was NOT tomato soup, despite the lingering aroma), our activity group headed to rock climbing.

I hate rock climbing.

Camp Mingle has a huge rock-climbing wall, one of those man-made deals with the little plastic toeholds attached randomly all over it. It's as high as our school and wide enough that three kids can climb at the same time. You might be thinking that skinny kids like me would make good climbers because we don't have much weight to carry, but you would be overlooking these scrawny arms with no muscles.

I delayed the inevitable as long as possible by insisting that my helmet didn't fit right and trying on almost every single one. Then I said my harness was pinching me, but once the climbing instructor got a look at my stick legs and found out that I'd tried on eighteen helmets, I got stuffed into the harness and was given a pep talk on courage.

Jessica has a tendency to abandon me in these situations. I like to think she's just excited about the activity – she loves this kind of thing – but she says it's because of the Whine Factor.

"That's it, you just sent the Whine Meter over 6.6. I'm outta here."

You'd think she could cut me some slack on the first day of camp, wouldn't you?

So, there I was in my harness and helmet, waiting with the few kids who had yet to climb. I was going to have to take my turn eventually. I watched as Jessica got her last-minute instructions and was hooked up to the rope. A boy named Dylan from St. Joe's was right beside her, watching. He was tall and strong-looking. He grinned at Jessica and jokingly asked if she wanted to race to the top of the wall.

"It's not a race, Dylan," the instructor said lightly. "We're just competing with ourselves, remember?"

Jessica rolled her eyes and nodded at Dylan. It was on!

Although the instructors released Dylan a second ahead of Jessica, she had obviously planned her first move. She leapt at the wall and was quickly even with Dylan. As the two of them climbed, kids from both schools cheered on their own classmate, drowning out the instructor's admonitions about not racing. By far the two fastest climbers in the group, Dylan and Jessica were neck and neck all the way up.

I heard the bell at the top of the wall and there was Jessica, swinging happily in her harness, first to the top. Dylan smiled down at his classmates, shrugged, and said, "Watch this."

He leaned back and began to repel down the wall. Most kids had done this part hesitantly or not at all, choosing instead to climb back down on the toeholds. But Dylan pushed away from the wall and let himself slide down the rope with confidence. It was impressive. He landed on his feet with a thud and turned to see Jessica already standing there. He hid his surprise quickly with a grin.

Since I was the last climber, everyone was watching. Sometimes stalling can backfire on you. It took me at least ten times as long as Jessica and Dylan. Jessica stood and urged me on as I struggled and gasped my way to the top, and by the time I got there, my arms were shaking so badly I could barely ring the stupid bell. I was lowered down by the instructor and hit the ground like a sack of dirt.

I couldn't even get the harness off. The instructor had to help me – while the whole group stood around waiting to be dismissed from the activity.

Humiliating.

As I walked away, I heard Dylan ask a kid what my name was.

"I think they call him Chuckie Cheese," the other kid said.

Camp was off to a great start.

CHAPTER 4

After supper (still no sign of any tomato soup), we all gathered at the firepit for games. One of the camp counsellors was building a fire for later. I liked the later part, sitting around the bonfire. Sometimes the leaders told stories, but usually we just sang goofy songs with crazy actions. And then we had hot chocolate and went to bed. Too bad we couldn't fast-forward past evening games.

The game for the first night was Capture the Flag, and the kids talked the counsellors into boys against the girls. What is it about boys vs girls that makes everyone so competitive? Once in fourth grade, we had a spelling bee and when the girls beat us, as usual, one of the boys freaked out and yelled, "Oh yeah? Well, let's see who can do the most push ups!" He actually got down on the classroom floor and started doing them. Not a proud moment for us guys.

I sat with the boys from my cabin and listened to them discuss strategy. I was thinking strategy too, but not about how to find the flag. Normally, this type of game is the perfect time for a sore ankle or maybe a bit of a cold. But after my humiliation at the climbing wall, I had to decide if my reputation would be damaged more by playing badly or by not playing at all.

In the end, I decided to employ one of my favourite strategies: *Look Busy and Don't Volunteer for Anything.* I had learned the hard way that standing around looking nervously unoccupied is the perfect way to be assigned a job by players who are so busy they need to employ other kids for some of their work. This is how you end up with hopelessly slow runners guarding the jail where captured prisoners await rescue. I mean, seriously!

I retied my shoelaces and watched out of the corner of my eye as Dylan mobilized the boys, assigning jobs to anyone who hadn't already shouted out what they were planning to do. I jumped up quickly but carefully – I got a wicked splinter in my butt from this bench last year – and ran toward the trees at the edge of the field, signalling assertively to my imaginary ally in the bush. I hoped I looked convincingly busy and strategic, then walked deep into the trees and started looking for a good spot to hide.

I sat on my patch of moss for so long that I was getting chilly by the time I spotted Dylan making his way slowly through the trees in enemy territory. No one had seen him yet, and he looked like he knew where he was going. By this stage of the game, enough reconnaissance information had been gathered that both sides would have a pretty good idea of where the opponent's flag was hidden. Sure enough, I lost sight of him for a second, and when I found him again, he was sprinting out into the open field carrying the flag with five girls in hot pursuit, Jessica included. He swerved back toward the treeline and started crashing through the bush, trying to shake off his pursuers. The rough terrain slowed most of the girls enough that they were no longer a threat to catch him, but Jessica was starting to gain on him.

Suddenly, she veered left to a clearing and drew even with him. She was three metres to his left when she stepped onto a fallen log and launched herself at him, diving through the air for the tag. I couldn't tell if she got him, but he didn't slow down. In seconds, he was back out into the open field, sprinting for home territory. The whole field erupted in cheers and groans as he dove across the line with girls closing in from all angles.

I looked for Jessica but couldn't see her, so I got up and started walking back to the fire circle; it was too soon to be seen consorting with the enemy, anyway. I puffed out my chest, slapped a few high fives, and joined in the general gloating.

When the edge between the teams had softened a bit, I decided it was safe to find Jessica. But she wasn't anywhere. I looked back at the field and saw a golf cart driving toward the spot where I'd seen her last. A small clump of girls stood watching the golf cart.

"What's going on?" I asked Lydia, a sixth-grader from St. Joe's. She was a friend of Jessica's from last year's camp.

"Jess hurt herself. I think it's pretty serious."

I started walking across the field, but the golf cart was already on its way back. I stopped and watched it make a wide arc around the fire circle and disappear into the bush on the off-limits side of the camp where all the staff cabins were.

I found Mr. George and asked if he knew what was happening. He gave me his usual look of vague annoyance, told me I could go see her at the nurse's cabin, and gave me directions. By the time I found it, Jessica was lying on a cot with one leg elevated on pillows, a cold pack wrapped around her ankle.

She looked happy to see me. I stood at the door of the tiny cabin which already contained three adults as well as Jessica; the two women were buzzing around her and the camp counsellor who had driven the golf cart was leaning against the wall like a limo driver.

"Should I wait outside?" I asked.

"No, dear," said Miss Blanchard. "Come right in. I'll leave you to keep Jessica company while I go call her mother. Now you're sure you're all right, Jessica? Can I leave you for a few minutes? Miss Lund will take good care of you." She indicated the camp nurse who was completely absorbed with the important task of arranging tensor bandages on the table in order of size.

"Pardon me?" Miss Lund asked, looking up when she heard her name. "Oh, yes. Go ahead. We'll be fine, won't we, Jessica? And who are you?" she asked, turning to me.

"I'm Charles," I said.

The driver and our agitated teacher left and I sat on a chair beside Jessica. I wasn't sure if the nurse was done talking to Jessica or not; she seemed completely focussed on the bandages.

"So, how does it feel?" I whispered to Jessica.

"It bloody hurts," she said. She was a nasty grey colour.

"Can I do anything?" I asked.

It was Miss Lund who answered. "Yes, thank you! The only bandage that is the right length for an ankle is still in the first-aid kit which just left on the golf cart. Could you run down and get it for me?"

Jessica moaned and turned her head toward the window. Just between you and me, I was happy to get out of there. I hate it when people are in pain. I don't even like to see the earthworms wiggling around trying to get back into the ground after a big rain. They look so uncomfortable and worried. I was halfway to the door when I heard another loud groan and then, "Chuck please don't leave me." I froze.

"Oh dear," said Nurse Lund. "Maybe you should stay with her, Chuck. She's fine; it's just a sprain, but it's such a comfort to have a friend..." She looked back and forth between the door and the patient. I had to assume this was her first gig.

"You go ahead; I'll stay," I said.

"I'll be back in five minutes." She patted Jessica on the shoulder and said, "There, there." I didn't know people actually said that, did you?

She flapped out the door and Jessica sighed loudly. "Thank goodness," she said happily.

"You faker!" I watched her face carefully. "It does hurt though, doesn't it?" I asked.

"Yes, it does. It's worse than when I broke my arm,

actually. Nurse Nervous said they have to talk to my mom before she can give me anything for the pain. My mom probably went all herbal on the medical form. My kingdom for a Tylenol." She grinned, but it was more of a grimace.

Jessica is way tougher than me. If it had been me, my ankle probably would have snapped clean off.

"I have to tell you something before Nurse Nutty gets back; I saw tents through the trees on the way here." She pointed at the south wall of the cabin. The nurse's cabin was the furthest one in this direction.

"I think it was probably the protestors' camp. The road is over there," she said pointing to the east wall. "And we could see the edge of the camp when we walked in, remember? I think we're just on the other side of their camp." She looked like her old self for a minute and I hated to disappoint her, but I didn't get why she looked so pleased.

"So?" I asked.

"So, we have the perfect opportunity for reconnaissance work here: volunteer to keep me company when Nurse Crazy isn't here, then you sneak over there and check things out. You can go spy on that guy and find out if he's your dad."

"Yeah, maybe," I said.

Then we both froze as we heard Miss Blanchard clear as day, right outside the door.

"Oh, hello dear, are you here to visit Jessica? How nice."

"Actually, I was just leaving," answered a familiar voice.

"Bye bye," Miss Blanchard sing-songed as she opened the cabin door.

She looked around. "Where's the nurse?"

"Went for a bandage," I heard Jessica say as I bolted past our teacher.

I rushed around the corner of the cabin just in time to see someone hurrying across the field. I flashed back to earlier, when I was watching Capture the Flag. I recognized those long strides. It was Dylan.

How much had he heard, if anything? He'd probably come to see how Jessica was and then didn't come in. Because he was eavesdropping? Or because he chickened out for some reason? Maybe he had a crush on Jessica.

I went back and hung around while Miss Blanchard told Jessica about the conversation with her mom, and when Miss Lund returned, the two adults stepped outside to talk privately.

I decided Jessica already had enough to deal with. She really was a ghastly colour. I wouldn't worry her with the Dylan mystery. I could see she was going to ask who'd been outside, so I talked before she had a chance to.

"You never told me what happened," I said, nodding at her ankle.

"I stepped on a mossy log when I dove for Dylan and my foot slipped and turned in the middle of my launch. I ended up pushing off on the outside of my ankle. But I tagged him, the little cheat. I felt the fabric of his shirt and then I felt pain. But I got him." She seemed satisfied with the trade-off of a sprained ankle for the knowledge that she caught him.

"Knock, knock," I said.

She groaned. "Gimme a break, Chuck – I'm in enough agony already without your terrible knock-knock jokes."

"Fine. I was trying to distract you from the pain."

She rolled her eyes. "Whatever, Chuck. Hey, you never told me who was outside before."

"Just some kid I didn't recognize. Probably looking for a bandage," I shrugged.

The cabin door opened while Jessica was eyeing me suspiciously – she can usually tell when I'm lying.

Miss Blanchard and Nurse Nutty were ready to update Jessica and the moment was lost in a wave of bad news.

Jessica had to sleep in the nurse's cabin the first night and would be on crutches for a while. They asked her if she wanted to go home, but she opted to stay at camp because she said the only thing worse than being on crutches is being on crutches with three older brothers. A couple of years ago when the eldest, Greg, broke his leg, the others hid his crutches, shortened them, lengthened them, made one long and one short, and put paint on the bottoms while he slept. Red and green. Greg's bedroom carpet still looks like a Twister game for little Christmas elves with exceptionally long arms.

Jessica had looked downright depressed when she told me about being on crutches all week. I thought of the plastic wrap in the bottom of my duffel bag which we'd never get to use.

On the other hand, maybe the prank would cheer her up. She and I had been planning it for months. We were going to sneak into the counsellors' washroom and plastic wrap the toilets. Hoping to give her something to laugh about, I decided to go ahead on my own with an adapted version of our plan.

I should probably explain that my friendship with Jessica was pretty much built on a foundation of practical jokes. This is ironic because it means that our friendship is built on deception, when, in fact, I have learned more about honesty from Jessica than from anyone else in my life.

I've known Jessica since the first day of kindergarten, but my first clear memory of her is from the spring of that year. April 1st.

April Fools' Day. The international holiday of pranksters.

We were having lunch and I just happened to be sitting beside Jessica. Everyone was opening their hippie lunch pails with all stainless-steel containers – a kid could get shunned for using plastic at CHS. When Jessica opened her first little container, I heard her gasp and leaned over to take a look. It was filled with sand. She took a second container out and opened it. Sand. All of her containers were filled with sand. There she sat with five little sand boxes sitting in front of her and I just felt awful for her. I thought I was going to throw up, I was so upset. Who would do such a cruel thing?

I knew she had three big brothers so that seemed like the obvious answer.

"Your brothers do that?" I asked her.

She didn't look that upset.

"Nope," she said. Inexplicably, she was grinning. "My mom! Good one!"

Jessica showed everyone, laughing with delight. I was still worried about the fact that she had no food and so I started to divide my lunch into two little piles while she showed off her great April Fools prank. Once everyone had seen it, she sat back down and looked around as if it was just now occurring to her that she had nothing to eat. I pushed the pile of food that I'd rationed from my own lunch toward her and her face lit up in a way that went straight to my chivalrous little five-year-old heart. While we ate, she chattered away about her family and their passion for pranking each other. I don't remember what she told me specifically, but from that day on we were friends and I loved hearing about the jokes her family played on each other. I also made sure I took extra lunch every April 1st because her mom still does something nuts to her lunch every single year.

I think part of the reason the prank culture at Jessica's house appeals to me is because it would never happen at my house. I'm an only child raised by a hippie mother with help from a gentle grandma and an uber-practical grandpa; nobody in that crowd would be laughing if I served them sand for lunch. Grandpa would want to take me to a shrink, Grandma would cry, and mom would whisper, "Oh Cedar, that is so harsh."

Meanwhile, over at Crazy Central, people were putting salt instead of sugar into the chocolate chip cookies, replacing jeans with younger sibling's jeans so the victim thought they were getting fat, hanging stuffies by the neck … it was endless. One of her brothers, Martin, went away to camp for a week and the rest of the kids spent the whole week setting up his bedroom in the garage. First, they drew it, mapping every piece of dirty laundry and moldy pizza, then they recreated it in the garage. It was an exact replica down to the last stinky gym sock.

I decided to get in on the action once and suggested that we put dye in the washing machine. Jessica looked at me like I was crazy. She sat me down and explained the Golden Rule of the prank: no irreversible damage – to people or their things.

That's why I thought a practical joke would cheer Jessica up. After all, it's a pretty huge bummer to sprain your ankle on the first day of camp when you look forward to camp all year.

So, on Monday night after all the boys were asleep, I waited until it got quiet. Mr. George slept in a tiny room which was separated from the main cabin by a door that was made of some sort of alien spaceship material that amplifies sound as it passes through. Even when we whispered as softly as possible, Mr. George would call, "I heard that!"

When I could hear him snoring, I snuck out of the cabin with my roll of plastic wrap under my arm. I had a flashlight with me, just in case, but I didn't want to attract the attention of anyone who might be out for some reason of their own.

It was one of those clear, still nights that are supposed to be more peaceful but can actually feel a little creepy if you're used to city sounds. There wasn't even a little breeze to rustle the trees for background noise. Nothing. Which meant every step I took on the gravel road towards the wash house sounded like an ogre chewing bones. My heart sped up. My feet sped up. I made more noise. I slowed down. I pictured the ogre. My heart sped up. My feet sped up.

Nearly hysterical, I broke into a run and sprinted down the road, imagining my feet were barely touching down at all and making no sound. When I got to the head of the two paths that went to either end of the wash house, I stopped and reminded myself as I caught my breath not to go right like I always did. I headed up the path to the left and tiptoed into the girls' bathroom. (No way was I sneaking into the counsellors' bathroom without a lookout.) I had never been in a girls' bathroom by choice before – being shoved in by the boys in first grade doesn't count. I have to admit, it was cleaner than ours.

I took out the wrap and unrolled a long piece. I lifted the seat of the first toilet and stretched the wrap tight across the top of the bowl with no wrinkles. I put the seat back down. No matter what angle I looked from, I couldn't see the wrap. Perfect.

Just as I headed into the second stall, I heard crunching. Someone was walking up the road!

I locked the door of the toilet stall and stood still, praying to whoever might be listening to make the walker go somewhere else. Then the crunching stopped, but I could hear footfalls on the path.

The girls' path.

My mouth went dry. *Get up on the toilet*, the working portion of my brain screamed. I climbed up carefully and placed one foot on either side of the seat. Stupid, lid-less toilets. I crouched down so my head wouldn't show over the top and braced myself against the walls. The footsteps entered the washroom and I held my breath. If the girls' washroom was anything like the boys', there was often a stall locked shut because the toilet wasn't working properly. I was okay there – she probably wouldn't be suspicious. But what if she went into the stall to my right? The one I had already booby-trapped?

I heard the door of the stall to the left open. My eyes rolled up in silent relief. It was then I noticed two things at the same time. My scrawny arms were starting to tremble from being braced against the walls to hold me still on my precarious perch. And that was making me sweat. Which was making my glasses start to slide down my nose. And at the end of my nose was a short dive to the toilet bowl.

I gritted my teeth. Don't move, don't sweat, don't breathe. Tilt head back.

The tinkling from next door stopped and I started praying again because there was no way my arms would hold out for a poop!

A rustling, a flush (during which I moved slightly and took a deep breath), then the door of the stall opening. Squeak of sink tap, water running, another squeak. Paper towel dispenser.

Almost there.

Then silence.

Did she float out? Or was she standing there looking at herself in the mirror? Or looking in the mirror at the stalls behind her? *Get out!* I silent-screamed at the risk of popping that blood vessel in my forehead.

My glasses slipped down again and I tilted my head back as far as I could. I could feel my left foot beginning to slide now. I wasn't going to make it. Both feet slid downward and I started to step off the toilet – just as the footsteps headed out the door and down the path.

I sank to my knees. Well, if I was going to upchuck from stress (wouldn't be the first time), I was in the right place.

Eventually, my breathing, heart rate, and queasy stomach all normalized. I went to the door and peeked out. It was all quiet. Except for my bunk calling softly to me.

Nope. I'd survived the worst. I had to finish. I covered every toilet in plastic wrap, listening so hard for footsteps that my eyes hurt. (Is it just me or do your eyes open super wide when you're listening really hard?) I double-checked them all from various angles to make sure nothing was noticeable. Then I stepped out into the oh-so-silent night and boogied back to my cabin.

My heart was still thumping a little when I finally

snuck back into bed. I was too hyped up from my mission to sleep. Even after I calmed down, my mind was flipping back and forth between the scene of mayhem in the girls' bathroom tomorrow morning and wondering whether or not I should take Jessica's advice and sneak over to the protest camp.

CHAPTER 5

Breakfast on Tuesday morning was fabulous. Definitely not because of the pancakes that tasted vaguely like tomato soup, but because of the night's successful porcelain sabotage. There was a lot of whispering, glaring, and finger-pointing going on.

Thought for the day: *Not a word to anyone (except Jessica).*

I've watched many great pranksters get caught because of their inability to keep their mouths shut. It is tempting, of course, because every artist wants to be acknowledged for their genius. But with pranksters – and secret agents – secrecy is the ultimate weapon.

I imagined great waterfalls of pee flooding the girl's washroom floor. I sat back and enjoyed all the whispering as the girls tried to figure out who knew, who the culprits were, and how to get their revenge.

The boys were equally entertaining, slowly clueing in to the story as they stuffed themselves with pancakes.

"Excuse me, campers," said the camp director, Mr. Garabaldi, or, as the kids like to call him, The Ear. He was short with very little hair on the top of his head but too much everywhere else. It even stuck out of the top of his t-shirt. Front and back. He was always twisting his left ear (also hairy) with his fingers, like he was trying to adjust the volume.

"There was a prankster out last night," Mr. Garabaldi said over the noise and the room went quiet. "We don't need to go into the details of the prank," he said and my chest accidentally puffed out a little. "But those responsible–and we know who they are–are all on report. Any more such pranks and those responsible will be sent home. The rules are about safety, campers. Wandering around after lights-out is not safe and will not be tolerated. Enjoy your pancakes."

I did enjoy my pancakes. They tasted like victory. *We know who they are.* Nice bluff, Ear! I couldn't wait to talk to Jessica, but she hadn't shown up for breakfast yet.

When she did come hobbling in on her crutches, I laughed out loud as soon as I saw her. Her bedhead looked like a bird was building a nest behind her right ear. "How was your night?" I asked.

"Lovely. If you like getting wakened every ten minutes by shooting pain."

"It hurt all night?"

"I had to sleep on my back with my foot up and I can't sleep on my back. Every time I rolled over in my sleep, it hurt my ankle and woke me up. I'm tired and cranky. Go get me a coffee."

I stood up. "No coffee for you. Can I interest you in some pancakes, Your Crankiness?"

When I returned with a plate of food, she sniffed it and said, "Why the heck do these pancakes smell like tomato soup?"

I passed her the maple syrup. "We have the low ropes course this morning. Are you coming to watch?"

"Maybe," she said around a mouthful of pancake.

I was glad when she decided to come, and we walked together to the ropes course. She was already getting the hang of her crutches, but we were still the last to arrive. Plus, I slowed us down with my detailed report on last night's mission. It didn't cheer her up the way I'd hoped, but she giggled when I acted out the morning scene I had imagined.

Once Jessica got settled on a log where she could watch the activity, Dylan came over, trailed by a small group of followers.

"Hi, Jess. How's your ankle doing? I heard you broke it."

Jessica gave him a smile that only I would recognize as fake. "Not broken, just a sprain. How's your conscience?"

I watched Dylan closely. I don't know what I was looking for, maybe a sign on his forehead that said: *I know your secret.* But he was a smooth customer and if he had heard us talking in the nurse's cabin, I didn't see any evidence of it.

Dylan leaned toward Jessica. "Did you say 'my conscience?'" He looked around at his groupies and laughed lightly.

"Yes," Jessica said. "If it was me, I would have 'fessed up to being tagged. But whatever." She shifted away from Dylan on the log.

"If you had tagged me, I would have said so. I hope

your ankle's better soon." He walked toward the counsellor who was trying to get us organized for the first event.

Being scrawny is generally a disadvantage in life, but every once in a while, there's a payoff. Being light and short is a definite advantage when it comes to balance. Assuming, of course, that you have some sense of balance to begin with, which I do. So last year at camp, I discovered I was great on the ropes course.

I sat with Jessica while I waited my turn and we analyzed everyone's style. Not in a mean way, just in a watching-to-learn way. Jessica was not great at ropes. She was better at speed things and I was better at concentration things.

When it was my turn, I stepped up carefully and gripped the rope. I wasn't even worried that I hadn't done this in a whole year.

I was awesome right up until the very end. It was only the low ropes so it wasn't a big deal that I fell. Dylan came and helped me up. He was actually being nice and then I heard Jessica's fake sneeze, the one where she pretends to sneeze loudly, but instead of saying "ah-choo," she says "a-hole."

On the way back to the dining room, she told me that Dylan had yanked on the rope when no one was looking and that's why I fell. "Aren't you mad, Chuck?" she said.

"You're mad enough for both of us. What's the matter with you?"

She stopped pegging and stared at me. "Seriously? I'm going on no sleep, my ankle kills, I can't do anything fun, my arms are starting to hurt already from these stupid crutches, and that Dylan creep has everyone convinced he's a great guy."

There was no point in saying anything; I knew she'd cool off soon enough.

Our activity group was the first back to the dining room for lunch so Jessica and I had our pick of tables. We chose one close to the kitchen with extra leg room for Madame Gimpy. We watched the parent volunteers putting pitchers of juice on all the tables. Kevin, one of the fifth-graders, was sitting alone at the next table, saving chairs for friends. When one of the pitchers was placed in front of him, I nudged Jessica.

"Watch this," I said, pointing to Kevin.

He was eyeing the jug of juice the way the teachers eye the clock on Friday afternoons.

"This should be good," Jessica said and settled herself more comfortably with her bad ankle propped up on an extra chair.

There are two things you need to know here. First, while the camp does provide juice, our City Hippie parents like to send their own concoction for us to drink. Vats of it. Healthy, organic "iced tea" made of hibiscus, rooibos, and home-pressed apple juice. Sound disgusting? Well, don't tell any of the adults I said so, but it's not. It's delicious and refreshing. By the end of the two weeks last year, the kitchen staff hardly bothered with the camp juice because nobody would drink it. Everyone was guzzling hippie tea. The camp's juice was some kind of powder you mix with water to create green, blue, or red fluorescent sugar-water.

The second thing you should know is that, while all of us CHS kids have been instructed by parents and teachers to drink our *own* juice, no one pays that much attention to who drinks what. But Kevin is on a no-sugar diet. I used to think his parents were just uber-hippies until the first time I saw what happens to him when he consumes sugar. It was an unfortunate incident involving mini-doughnuts at a Christmas skating party. Let's just say no one needed stitches so it ended all right.

Anyway, Kevin is monitored closely when it comes to sugar intake, and it has nothing to do with hippie or not. In fact, Kevin's family is the least hippie family at CHS.

But the adults were all busy getting lunch ready and he was starting to look a bit crazed. Then he snapped. We watched him guzzle three glasses of glow-in-the-dark juice before moving to another chair in front of a jug of hippie tea. Jessica and I looked at each other. "Wait for it," she said.

We were distracted from the Sugar Games when the main door of the dining hall burst open and another activity group was herded in by Mr. George.

He spotted Kevin sitting alone at his table, then noticed the half-empty radioactive juice jug.

"Did you drink that?" he barked at Kevin.

"No, it was like that when I got here," Kevin said. His toe was tapping like a drum roll under the table.

Mr. George narrowed his eyes and turned to us. "Did he drink that?"

Jessica and I both shrugged. I used my *concerned, but unable to assist* face, and Jessica used her *couldn't care less* face.

The rest of the kids all showed up at once, and in the craze of getting two plates of food, I lost track of Kevin.

Nurse Lund stopped by our table partway through lunch to remind Jessica she was due back at the nurse's cabin at one o'clock for "icing and elevation." Afternoon activities didn't start until two, so I went with Jessica to keep her company. As we left the dining room, we heard a huge crash and a bunch of people yelling, "Ke-vin!!"

On the way to the nurse's cabin, Jessica didn't talk for the first while as she concentrated on her crutch rhythm. Most people would be satisfied with simply moving forward, but not Jessica. Once she was swinging along with maximum efficiency, she started in on me.

"This is our chance, Chuck. Miss Lund is still in the dining room, so we have some time on our own. I'll ice; you sneak through the woods and check out the protest camp."

I didn't answer her. I hadn't decided what to do about Jessica's plan. When I thought about the man who looked like me, I certainly felt something like excitement, but when I focused on it, I couldn't tell if my anxious feeling was the anticipation kind or the worried kind. Which probably meant it was a bit of both.

We were across the grass and into the trees when Jessica's voice cut into my thoughts.

"Earth to Chuck, come in, Chuck!"

"Maybe you'd get a response if you used my real name."

"That attitude right there is why no one should ever be named after a king." Jessica stopped and turned around awkwardly on her crutches. "Seriously, CHARLES, are you gonna go or what?"

"Yes, and I had already planned to go, so don't think you're the boss of me, Tripod," I lied.

She turned around and continued stumping.

At the nurse's cabin, I quickly helped her get her leg set up with the ice and then I scooted out the door and into the trees.

All I had for navigation was Jessica's vague pointing, so I headed off in that direction. I was good with this kind of thing in the city and never got lost, but these trees all looked alike. I tried to notice ones that were forked, or looked burnt, or were particularly huge. I was so busy watching for landmarks, I was zigging and zagging. Which is fine in the city – one block north, one block east – but there were no street signs here. Or streets. Or anything that ran in a straight line. My zig-zag pattern could be taking me in absolutely any direction, depending on the length of the zig as opposed to the zag. What was I doing out here?

Just when I started to worry that I was going to get lost, spend the night in the forest, and be eaten by wolves, I spotted the camp through the trees.

There was a big clearing with a firepit in the centre and I got as close to that as I could. There were logs around it for seats, and beyond that, there was a table under a big tarp. There were camp stoves, coolers, lanterns, and big jugs of water. I wasn't near enough to hear what anyone was saying, but I had a decent view of the dozen or so people milling about. Everyone wore rubber boots even though it was sunny and warm, as though the dry ground could betray them at any time.

The rest of the camp was beyond the clearing. From where I was hiding, I could count eight tents, splashes of colour here and there in the woods. There were probably more that I couldn't see.

I shifted my position and looked around at the bushes I was crouching in. It occurred to me that I couldn't identify poison ivy to save my butt. That was a joke, in case you're wondering.

I sat as still as possible and watched people chop wood and tidy the kitchen area. A couple of women stood chatting next to the road where three men sat in lawn chairs. By the looks of things, protesting was pretty boring.

I looked more closely at the camp itself. There were a lot of wires. At first, I assumed they were attached to the various poles holding up the tents and shelters, but when I actually followed them with my eyes, they went way up into the trees. There were platforms up there and that's what the guy wires were connected to. People were living in the trees! Well, that was one way to make sure no one cut them down.

I studied the platform closest to my hiding spot. It looked to be six feet wide and the same long, built in the first elbow of a huge tree, about twenty-five feet off the ground. Mesh bags hung around the edges of the platform and a bucket attached to a rope sat on the ground directly beneath it.

While I checked out the platforms, someone came running out of the trees from the tents. It was the guy we'd seen on Monday. I squinted and pushed up my glasses until they were denting the bridge of my nose. He *did* look like me. He ran toward the road and everyone else started running too.

I stepped cautiously through the bush and took a few steps toward the road where a large truck approached. Out of the corner of my eye, I glimpsed someone moving as if he did not want to be seen. I crouched down and watched a person in a black hoodie circling the camp.

Why would someone be skulking around a protest camp? The options that came to me – FBI, for example – were a clear indication that I watched too many movies. But really, why would someone not want to be seen unless they were up to no good? When the black hoodie had gone all the way around the main clearing of the camp, it started moving toward the tents.

I stayed still as a statue, barely breathing, until I couldn't see the black hoodie anymore. Then, I sprinted back toward Camp Mingle, hoping I was going in the right direction.

I didn't slow down until I got to the nurse's cabin, where I waited until my heart was beating normally again before pulling open the door. Jessica was alone.

"What happened?" she asked. "Your eyes are big as frisbees!"

"Did Nurse Lund come?" I asked.

"Just once – to get a butterfly bandage for someone who ran into the flagpole while being chased by a mob of angry girls. Guess who?"

"Kevin."

"Yup. Don't worry. I told her you went to the bathroom. What happened?" she asked again.

"There was this guy sneaking around the camp. I nearly ran into him."

Jessica frowned at me. "What do you mean 'sneaking?' Wasn't he from their camp?"

"I don't know. But he definitely didn't want any of them seeing him. He was wearing a black hoodie!"

"So?" Jessica leaned forward too quickly and grimaced.

"So, remember the black hoodie we saw in that old mossy car? It must have been the guy who's living there."

She flopped back onto the pillows behind her. "Did you see the guy who looks like you?"

And then I made one of those split-second decisions you can't explain.

"No," I told her. "I never saw him."

CHAPTER 6

Our afternoon activity was swimming, and by the time Jessica and I got to the beach, the rest of our group was already there – had been for most of the free hour, in fact, because it was hot. As I helped Jessica get settled on a towel, I could hear Dylan entertaining everyone with his eye-witness account of Kevin's run-in with the flag pole.

Once the lifeguard gave the okay, everyone else – except Jessica and me – plunged into the lake. I stood at the edge with my feet in the cool water and tried to imagine myself as tanned and muscular. I hitched up my baggy bathing suit.

On the deep side of the dock, kids pulled each other off inner tubes and air mattresses. On the shallow side, Dylan and a few others were standing in the water playing catch with a frisbee.

"Hey, Chuckie Cheese, wanna play?" a kid from St. Joe's asked. There's a dilemma for you: cool group invites you to join them using derogatory nickname; what do you do?

"Sure," I said and waded out a bit deeper. I stayed in the shallowest part because I can't swim. I believe that this is because of the scrawniness factor, as well. Next time you're at the beach, watch for the good swimmers;

they usually have an extra layer of fleshy buoyancy help-
ing them. Just a theory, but seriously, I sink like a rock.

I inched out until the water was up to my knees.
The sun felt great on my back. I am a big fan of summer
days and this was a beauty. I was far more interested
in my surroundings than I was in tossing a plastic disc
around. The trees watched over us like extra lifeguards,
the hidden birds whistling at our rowdy behaviour. A
metallic blue damselfly landed on the shoulder of the
kid next to me and I leaned in to get a closer look.

Whap! Frisbee to the head. I rubbed my temple and
looked around at the laughing circle of kids as though
I'd just noticed them. The next time a kid threw it to
me, they yelled my name first to make sure I was ready.
Well, they yelled *a* name.

Dylan tossed the disc to the kid across from me
who had to dive for it, launching himself out fearlessly
into the lake. He came up sputtering and laughing and
then everyone was missing each other on purpose to see
who could create the most spectacular dives. Everyone
but me. I don't like my head being under water. The
guy right next to me made an amazing dive, which was
actually a belly flop, and when everyone was finished
laughing, Dylan suggested we move out a bit deeper so
belly flops wouldn't hurt so much. I was a little nervous
as the circle slowly edged out deeper and deeper, but I
was enjoying myself so much, I barely noticed.

"Charles!"

Jessica's voice was loud and urgent. I spun around
to look at her and she was rolling around on her towel,

clutching her ankle. I hurried out of the water and ran up the beach. "What happened?" I asked, as I helped her sit up.

"I tried to get up and it twisted in the sand," she said, looking toward the water. I turned to see the frisbee game had come to a halt.

"Everything okay?" Dylan called.

"Yes, she's all right," I called back and the game resumed.

Jessica whispered, "What a jerk!"

I thought she was talking about me at first. "What?"

"Dylan, with his subtle little tactics. I hate that guy!"

"What are you talking about?" I looked back at the group to see what she saw – I had no idea why she was upset.

"He was slowly pulling the circle out further and further, trying to embarrass you."

It took me a second to put it all together. "Wait, did you fake-hurt yourself?"

"Yes! I had to get you out of there before he could embarrass you for not being able to swim."

I was annoyed with her for interrupting the most fun I'd had at camp so far, but I didn't know how to respond to her. When in doubt, use humour.

"Thought for the day, Jessica: *Paranoia will destroy ya!*"

"Chuck, wake up. Dylan was trying to humiliate you."

"He doesn't even know I can't swim!" I was getting exasperated.

"Don't count on it," she said and sat there staring daggers at him.

I plopped down on the sand beside her because I didn't know what else to do. The frisbee circle had broken up and the kids were all in the deeper part of the lake. If I went back in now, I'd be the loser standing alone in ankle-deep water.

I was considering stalking off in a huff when Jessica turned to me like nothing had happened and asked if I wanted to go play chess on the giant board you can walk on. I was still angry, but chess was better than sitting here baking in the sun, looking at the water I couldn't swim in. Besides, watching Jess try to play on crutches would probably cheer me up.

We got the lifeguard to sign us out of the activity group by saying that I was taking Jessica to the nurse's cabin. By the time we got up to the courtyard outside the dining hall, I was feeling slightly better and decided to forget about it. Hopefully, she would let it go too.

It was actually a good thing to do because playing chess is one of the few times Jessica is quiet. She mutters a bit as she studies the board, but just to herself. Sometimes I wonder if I've gone invisible when I play chess with Jessica. She rarely beats me, but she believes every single time that she can win. By the time we finished two games, both of which I won, I was feeling much better.

That night after dinner, we used Jessica's injury as an excuse to get out of Fort Knox and that suited me fine. I hate that game. Jessica and I sat on the benches at the firepit and watched everyone running around like crazy people. I don't actually know what crazy people look like when they run around, but I imagine it would be similar to a bunch of kids playing Fort Knox.

"Whatcha thinking about?" Jessica asked after a particularly long and peaceful silence.

"I was wondering about that guy I saw at the camp. You know, Black Hoodie Guy. Why was he sneaking around like that?"

"Maybe he was supposed to be looking for little snoops from Camp Mingle but sucks at his job."

"He was hiding from the protestors. If he didn't want to be seen, why was he so close to their camp?"

"Maybe he was stealing from them. Or planning to."

"Maybe," I said. But I wasn't listening to Jessica. The guy in the hoodie creeped me out and I was thinking about whether I'd be brave enough to go back to the camp knowing he was out there. What was I more afraid of? Black Hoodie Guy? Or never knowing if my look-alike was actually my father?

CHAPTER 7

On Wednesday morning, we had archery. Jessica wolfed down a plate of tomato soup-flavoured scrambled eggs and then nagged me while I finished mine.

"I can *do* this one. Let's go."

I didn't want to discourage her, so I didn't say anything, but standing squarely with your weight evenly distributed on both legs is an important part of archery. I wasn't so sure she'd be able to do it.

The range was one of my favourite places at camp. Not just because I was good at archery, but because the trees there were huge and old and had moss hanging from their limbs like the fringed suede jacket my mom occasionally digs out of the closet. Things hanging from limbs should definitely be restricted to trees.

For obvious reasons, the archery range was a long way from anything else and there was nothing behind the targets but trees. I can only imagine how many arrows live in the forest now. The archery instructor makes you search a long time if you overshoot the target, but eventually they call off the search and another arrow settles into life in the wild.

Each of the six targets was a metre across and had its own wooden shooting platform twenty-five metres in front of it. There was a wall of hay bales behind each target. Other than the platforms, targets, and bales, everything else in the area was forest. It made me feel like Robin Hood.

Last year, I had to use the small bow set. I was looking forward to using the large one this year, with its extra power and accuracy. We lined up for sizing and Jessica and I chatted about aiming strategies. I finally got to the front of the line where my next humiliation awaited; every sixth-grader and most of the fifth-graders got to use the large bows, but not me.

We sat on a huge, mossy log with a line of kids and waited for our turn. We told knock-knock jokes till we got to the front of the line. When it was Jessica's turn, I watched her wobble all over the place without her crutches, trying to get steady on her sore ankle. I'm sure it hurt, but she managed to shoot pretty well. I kept my eye on the targets, praying the one with the smaller bow would be the next one available. But, of course, it wasn't. Another one opened up – with a large bow – and before I could tell the girl beside me to go ahead, Dylan called from the far end of the log, "Hey Chuck, you're up, dude."

My face went totally red and I stammered something about waiting for the next one. I told the girl beside me to go.

"Why?" She looked at me suspiciously.

"I'll wait for the next target." I thought my face was going to burst into flames it was so hot.

"Chuck, let's go!" Dylan called again from the end of the log.

"Go!" the girl beside me urged.

I looked at the ground in front of the girl. "I have to wait for the smaller bow set," I whispered.

"Oh, okay," she said as she hopped off the log.

"What's up?" Dylan yelled.

"He has to wait for the small bow," she yelled back.

I wanted to die. I glanced at Jessica for some moral support and she was glaring at Dylan. She looked mad enough to pin him to the target with one of her regular-sized arrows.

I hesitated for a moment, weighing my humiliation in one hand and my love of archery in the other. If I could shoot well, perhaps this moment would be forgotten. So, I took my turn and I did shoot well. I loved every part of archery: lining it up carefully, the tension of the bowstring when you pull it back as far as it will go. And my favourite part is the sound the arrow makes when you let it go and it hits the target. *Zoop. Thunk.*

I also enjoy the sound of other people's arrows hitting the bales of hay. Or the extra long *zoooop* when an arrow misses the target and the bales and heads out to search for relatives in the forest.

By the end of the morning, the small bow fiasco seemed to have been forgotten by everyone except Jessica. All the way back to the dining hall, she tried to convince me that Dylan had meant to embarrass me.

"Jeez, Jessica, will you let it go? You sound like a nut job; somehow Dylan *knows* that I need the small bow. And that I can't swim! Enough, already." But she wouldn't stop with her conspiracy theories, so I sped up and left her clumping far behind me. It was beginning to feel like *she* was the one trying to ruin camp for me.

To avoid her at lunch, I sat in the last available chair at a table in the back corner of the dining room. By the end of the meal, I had cooled off, but when I went to find her, the girls at her table told me she'd gone to the arts and crafts pavilion with Lydia's activity group.

Our group was doing canoeing, so I hurried down to the beach before all the new life jackets were gone. The older ones were a lot bulkier and hotter to wear, and the sun was blazing. For a non-swimmer, I actually like boats. I feel safe in a PFD – that means personal flotation device – and I'd been in canoes before and never dumped. But I didn't want to, either. Because of the head-under-water thing. So, I was looking around for a responsible-looking partner when Dylan came up.

"Hey Chuck, how's it going?" he asked.

I hesitated a second, then said quickly, "I prefer Charles, actually."

"Okay, Charles, you want to be my partner for canoeing?"

I looked at him carefully, feeling a sliver of Jessica's paranoia under my skin. I ignored it.

"Okay." I tried to sound casual with a hint of bore-dom, but it came out, well, scrawny.

The safety lesson was quick, even with Mr. George interrupting every few minutes when he thought the bored instructor had missed an important point. Apparently, Mr. George was missing being Lord of the Gym.

"So, would you recommend standing in the canoes?" Mr. George looked very pleased with himself.

"Oh, right: NEVER stand up in a canoe," said the instructor, stifling a yawn.

(Lights out at ten o'clock around this place, but the camp counsellors always looked like they'd gotten about twenty minutes of sleep.)

Once Mr. George had exhausted his supply of helpful questions, we were turned loose.

"So, which way do you want to go?" Dylan asked from the rear of the canoe.

We weren't allowed to go outside a certain area, but it was big. As long as we could see the lifeguard in her little yellow zodiac, we were okay.

"I don't care," I said, hoping he'd go south toward the protest camp. There probably wasn't much to be seen from shore, but it was worth a look.

"Okay, how about we check out that little bay there?"

I turned around carefully to see where he was pointing. North. Oh well.

None of us knew what we were doing and all the matching red canoes lurched away from the launch area like bumper cars. I was glad to be moving away from the pack, at least. We zig-zagged our way along. I didn't say anything about Dylan's steering, but it was bad.

We wobbled along the shoreline and eventually began to round the point into the bay. I looked back to see if I could still see the lifeguard's yellow boat just as it disappeared from my view. I figured we'd take a quick look around the bay and paddle out again. No harm done.

Suddenly, the canoe tipped hard to the right. My heart jumped and I slammed my paddle down flat in front of me, bracing it across the boat. I sat as still as I could.

"Sorry, Charles. I must have moved too quickly. That didn't make you nervous, did it?"

"No problem," I said, but my heart was still pounding.

I didn't move, but Dylan took a couple more strokes and now I couldn't even see any of the other canoes.

"We should probably head out of the bay or the lifeguard will be after us," I said over my shoulder.

"Okay," Dylan said, and the canoe started to turn. I wasn't sure which side to paddle on to help us turn, but I picked the right one and we circled around.

And then I was in the water. Honestly, it happened that fast. I have no idea how I fell out, but I did.

I'd like to tell you that I was calm and trusted my PFD, blah, blah, blah.

Nope.

As soon as I was under water, I panicked. I must have yelled because I swallowed water and started choking and kicking and thrashing and my paddle was gone and I didn't even know which way was up and which was down and my heart was pounding like a galloping horse and my lungs were burning and my brain was screaming, "AIR!!"

And then, I could breathe again. I took a big gulp of beautiful air, but it made me cough more. I was still choking, but at least my head was above water. I felt someone pull my arm onto the side of the canoe, so

I grabbed on with both hands and kept coughing and blinking to clear my eyes. I couldn't see because of the water on my glasses – thank goodness they'd stayed on my face. When I could breathe again, I squinted up to see Dylan reaching over me from the inside of the canoe, holding onto my PFD.

"Just hang on, Charles; you're okay," he said.

I sputtered some more and finally caught my breath. And as soon as I calmed down, I got embarrassed. I tried to remember if I'd screamed but had no idea. Let me tell you, panic is a horrible thing. The more I remembered, the more humiliated I felt. I couldn't look at Dylan, who was still hanging on to me.

"I'm okay. You can let go," I mumbled.

"You sure?" he asked.

I nodded glumly.

"Okay," he said. "I'm gonna paddle us out to where I can signal the lifeguard. You just hang on to the canoe."

I was trying not to cry now. I was embarrassed and shaky and scared and upset. By the time the lifeguard came and dragged me into the zodiac like a sack of wet laundry, I was shivering.

The lifeguard made all the canoes come into shore while she was not available to watch them, so there was a nice, big audience when we arrived with me shaking like a bird in a blizzard. The lifeguard wrapped me in a towel like a five-year-old and asked me a bunch of questions to see if I was okay.

Mr. George took me to the nurse's cabin, and after I finally warmed up, they made me lie down and rest.

Mr. George told the nurse Dylan's version of what had happened.

Apparently, we both leaned out to paddle on the same side at the exact same time and the canoe tipped way over. I fell in, but Dylan saw me going over, threw his weight in the opposite direction, and hung on.

Mr. George wanted to know what happened when I was in the water. I sat up and told him, skimming quickly over the part where I panicked. When I mentioned that I couldn't swim, he went a bit pale.

"You realize you might have drowned? Dylan may have saved your life."

I nodded. To tell you the truth, I thought Mr. George was making a slightly bigger deal than necessary. I'm sure I would have calmed down eventually and found the canoe. How can you drown in a PFD? Isn't that the point of wearing one? But Dylan did "rescue" me and you never know what might have happened.

"Can I go now? I feel fine."

Miss Lund gave me another once-over and let me go.

I didn't want to go back to the beach, so Mr. George let me go to the arts and crafts pavilion to find Jessica. She was coming out the door with Lydia as I arrived.

"Chuck, are you okay? I heard you almost drowned. What the heck happened?" Jessica leaned forward, gripping her crutches with her armpits so she could grab my shoulders with her hands and give me a little shake. She peered into each eye like she was checking for seaweed.

I pulled away and sighed. The whole camp probably knew by now.

"I heard Dylan saved your life. Everyone's talking like he's a superhero. What really happened? Come. Sit." She waved goodbye to Lydia, stumped over to a picnic table, and plopped down.

"Our canoe started to dump and I fell out. Dylan grabbed me and pulled me back to the canoe. That's all."

"What do you mean the canoe started to dump?" she asked.

"It started to tip. We were turning and we were both paddling on the same side and I guess we both reached out our paddles at the same time and leaned too far and the canoe started to tip. Dylan grabbed on and stayed in; I fell out."

"What was he doing before you tipped?"

I frowned at her. "I don't know. I don't have eyes in the back of my head."

"He was behind you?" she asked.

"Yes!" I was starting to get cranky.

"Chuck, canoes don't tip *that* easily. He must have done it on purpose."

"It's Charles," I said through gritted teeth. "And canoes tip all the time. That's why half the lesson was about how not to tip your canoe. Let it go, Jessica!"

She was quiet for a minute. Then she asked me who else had been there.

"What do you mean?" I asked.

"Who was in the canoe closest to you?"

"We were in a bay – we couldn't see the others."

She gaped at me. "Holy smokes, Chuck! He paddles you away where no one can see and you mysteriously tip and he gets to be the camp hero? How can you not see what a creep this guy is?"

"And how can you not see that you're the only one who thinks that? You weren't there so you don't know what happened. He didn't do it on purpose and he was nice to me." I could hear the anger in my voice.

When she didn't say anything else, I got up to leave.

"Are you still going to keep me company during games tonight?" she asked.

"Yes," I said, but only because I'd already promised her I would.

CHAPTER 8

That evening, when the campers convinced the counsellors to let them have a rematch of Capture the Flag instead of the planned game, Jessica got up from the bench we were sitting on and grabbed her crutches.

"Where are you going?" I asked.

"I can't watch. Let's do some more reconnaissance."

It was dusk and I didn't feel good about the possibility of running into Black Hoodie Guy in the dark. Plus, I was too worn out from my stupid accident to go traipsing through the woods. I was even too tired to explain it to Jessica. I decided to go with her to the nurse's cabin for now and make an excuse later.

We found Nurse Lund sitting inside the dining hall having tea with the kitchen staff.

"Is it okay if Chu – Charles and I go to your cabin to ice my ankle?" Jessica asked.

"Yes, of course, dear. Good for you, taking such initiative in your own recuperation. I'll be right with you."

"No, that's okay," Jessica smiled her fake smile. It was convincing. "Charles can help. You finish your tea."

I nodded and tried to look responsible. Miss Lund looked back and forth between us and smiled a little uncertainly. "Yes, you'll be fine, won't you? I'll be up in a bit."

"You don't need to worry about us. We'll make sure the lights are out and the door is closed tight when we leave." Jessica always knew what to say.

Miss Lund settled in her chair and waved us away happily.

As soon as we were inside the cabin, Jessica started scheming.

"If you go right now, you could be there and back before it gets totally dark. Take your flashlight, though. Do you have it with you?" she asked, without looking at me. She was studying her watch. "Make sure you're back in an hour and we can slide in with the hot chocolate crowd. If Nurse Neurotic shows up, should I say you went to the bathroom?" She finally realized I was not synchronizing my watch or searching for my flashlight or putting camouflage paint on my face. I was standing there staring at her.

"What's with you?" she asked.

"I'm kinda tired. Big day. Near-death experience and all." I made a goofy face I didn't feel.

Jessica looked at me for a moment, then shrugged and pulled out the deck of cards the nurse kept in a basket under the window. I helped her get set up at the table with her leg elevated and we started playing double solitaire without talking. I relaxed and forgot about being angry with Jessica and about the two mystery men out in the woods. One seemed to be a pretty suspicious character and the other might be my father. You'd think I would be more frightened about meeting Black Hoodie Guy, but you'd be wrong.

When we were half way through a second game of double solitaire, Jessica started in about Dylan again while I ignored her, concentrating on the game and not responding. But she wouldn't take the hint. She babbled away about what a jerk he was, wondering why he had it in for me. Finally, I couldn't take it anymore. I decided I'd rather face an axe-murderer than listen to her. I cut her off in mid-sentence.

"I'm gonna go check things out at the camp. Cover for me?"

She blinked at me with her mouth still in mid-flight. "Uh, sure," she said.

I grabbed my flashlight and was out the door before she could say anything else.

Being angry kept me warm and focussed as I stomped through the trees thinking about what a pain in my butt Jessica was being about Dylan. It made no sense to me. She seemed to be the one to have it in for Dylan.

Then – I tripped over a root and nearly did a header, so I switched on the flashlight, shielding the beam as best I could. It had quickly gotten dark. And chilly too. And a bit freaky. I shivered and looked around to make sure I knew where I was. Maybe doing this in the dark wasn't such a good idea. But I recognized the big tree that looked like it had been struck by lightning and headed towards it.

This was very different than navigating during the day. I was starting to get a bit nervous, not just about whether I could see well enough not to get lost, but about the way things change in the dark. The way you see things out of the corner of your eye. The way shadows become thicker and start to look like they have a life of their own.

With the sound of my heart humming in my ears, I moved ahead, scanning right and left for the glow of a campfire. When I finally spotted it, my breath rushed out of me and I slowed down to be as quiet as possible. I switched off my flashlight and took one careful step at a time.

The whole protest camp appeared to be around the fire, talking. They were so loud I was able to get even closer than the day before and I settled behind a big tree where I could hear everything but was completely invisible in the dark forest.

Before the light disappeared from the sky completely, I set my course back to Camp Mingle in my head. I'd be okay.

I tuned in to the babble at the fire and tried to sort it into separate voices. Bits of various conversations floated past me.

"...kill me if he knew. He thinks I'm still at college and...

"...asked her a million times to wash and refill the water bottles she brings back and she keeps dumping them in the sink and...

"...but training the loggers about sustainable practices was too expensive, so the plan fell apart before we..."

One voice rose above the rest. It came from a guy sitting on the side of the circle closest to my hiding spot.

"Hey Shell, tell the newbies your story from Nipkin Bay."

Shell.

My heart sped up so fast it felt like there was a rabbit in my shirt. A guy who looked like me. The name Shell. That was too much to be a coincidence, wasn't it? Yet, my brain demanded evidence. Were Shell and the guy who looked like me the same person? I strained to pick out the voice that responded to the loud guy, but it was impossible. All I heard was the blended babble of the group. I sat as long as I could on the cold, hard ground, but eventually had to move. It was pitch-black and I needed to get back before I was missed.

I carefully made my way back through the woods. I probably turned on my flashlight a bit sooner than I should have, but I was getting nervous. I'm not afraid of the dark, but anyone with a brain knows how easy it is to get lost in the woods at night.

I got back to the nurse's cabin, pushed open the door, and stepped into the warmth and light.

Jessica looked relieved. "I was starting to worry you'd run into Hoodie Man."

"No sign of him," I said, as I pulled a chair up to the table.

The door opened and Miss Lund walked in. "Oh Charles, you're back," she said. She put something on the table and, while her back was turned, Jessica started gesturing at me like we were playing charades. Unfortunately, I'm terrible at charades.

"So, how'd it go?" Miss Lund smiled at me.

"Uh, it went fine," I said, face flaming. Was that a normal question to ask someone when they returned from the bathroom? I glanced at Jessica who bit her lip and looked at the ceiling.

"Feeling better now?" Miss Lund inquired sympathetically.

I stared at her blankly.

"It does feel good to get it out, doesn't it?" Miss Lund asked.

"Um, I guess so." I thought my head was going to explode.

Jessica was making her "yikes" face. Perhaps Miss Lund and I were not discussing my trip to the bathroom after all.

This sort of situation can almost give me an allergic reaction. Miss Lund was looking back and forth between me and Jessica, and her expression was changing quickly.

"Where were you Charles?" she asked firmly.

Well, obviously not at the bathroom. What the heck had Jessica told her? *How'd it go? Did I feel better?* I was drawing a complete blank, and she was waiting for an answer.

"I went for a walk," I blurted. "Just around. Uh. On the path. And to the field. To watch the game. Capture the Flag…" I fizzled out when she put her hands on her hips and lowered her chin. What is it with adults? Can they smell lies?

"Were you outside the camp boundaries, Charles?"

She was looking through my skull into my brain. Confessing was the only way to get her out of there.

"Maybe a little," I said.

By the time the director was finished with me, it was late and he sent me to bed so I didn't see Jessica until breakfast. I was tempted to sit somewhere else and ignore her completely, but she was waving like a lunatic when I walked in. She pointed to the chair she'd saved for me.

"What happened with the director?" she asked before I was all the way into my seat.

"I got a long lecture and a warning. If I get caught off the grounds again, I get sent home. That's what happened with the director. What happened with your brain?"

"I know, I know," she groaned. "When Nurse Nosey first came in, I told her you went to the bathroom, but after half an hour, I had to say something so I told her you'd mentioned needing to talk to your counsellor about your near-death experience because you were upset."

I stared at her. "Are you crazy?"

"I know. I panicked. Plus, who'd have thought she'd walk back in right after you did? I didn't have time to explain. If it happens again, I'll say you're sick, okay?"

"If it happens again? Do you know what my mom would do if I got kicked out of camp and she had to take time off work and borrow a car and … there won't be a next time, Jessica!"

"Okay, I get it." Jessica stared at her nasty lump of oatmeal. "You *were* gone a long time," she said quietly.

I looked at her. "So, it was my fault? Do you know how hard it is to walk through bush with no flashlight?" I was getting angry again.

"You had a flashlight!"

"I couldn't use it anywhere near the camp; they would have seen me!"

"Oh, yeah," she said quietly.

And that was it. No apology for making up such a stupid story and leaving me hanging. I built a castle with a moat in my oatmeal while I thought about who I was going to sit with at lunch time. Thought for the day: *Find a new best friend.*

Thursday morning was our group's turn for arts and crafts. I was still mad and I was busy getting a head start on worrying: if I survived making this stupid macramé plant hanger, the afternoon's activity was kayaking and I was nervous. My last boating experience was not exactly enjoyable.

I worried my way through arts and crafts, worried back to the cabin and into my swimsuit. As I stood worrying on the beach, Pacific asked if I wanted to go in a double kayak with him and I froze. I stared at him, wondering if it would be better to be in a single or double kayak if something went wrong. In the end, I decided I'd feel safer if I only had to worry about myself. By the time I finally said, *No, thank you*, Pacific had already wandered away.

I chose a trustworthy-looking boat, just enough scratches and dents to suggest *experience*, not enough to suggest *leak*. I felt anxious for the first while, but, by the time the lesson was over, I was feeling more comfortable. Of course, I was sitting exactly in the middle of my boat and I was slow because I didn't want to reach out too far with the double-bladed paddle. I floated around close to the swimming area and, as I got more confident, I ventured further out. But I made sure I could still see the yellow zodiac.

I went south along the shore, peering into the woods. After a few minutes, I thought I saw something moving on a little, rocky beach. I pulled closer to shore and paddled toward the blob which turned out to be a person. A person bent over at the waist as though looking for something in the sand and pebbles.

A person wearing a black hoodie.

He straightened suddenly and walked quickly into the trees.

The hair was standing up on the back of my neck. Literally. Like a dog with its hackles raised. There was no question now: I was not going anywhere near the woods again. I felt relieved once I said that to myself. Relieved because I didn't want to run into Hoodie Guy – ever.

Also relieved because I wasn't a rule-breaking kind of guy and my recent crime spree was giving me stomach aches. But mostly relieved about not meeting Shell, in case he was a jerk.

After all, my fantasy dad was perfect and let me do anything I liked – even cut my hair. Why mess with perfection?

CHAPTER 9

Thursday night was a break from games because it was our planning session for the big event on Saturday evening: Talent Night.

Talent Night was a time-honoured tradition, blah, blah, blah.

I'll tell you what Talent Night is: it's an introvert's worst nightmare.

On Thursday and Friday, you get together to plan and practise, and on Saturday, you face public humiliation by standing in front of the entire camp to do something you would NEVER normally do. I hate things like this. As if my life didn't have enough public humiliation built right in.

Our group was meeting in the arts and crafts pavilion, which was also the storage area for all the sports equipment and the main back-up space for rainy days. Basically, the pavilion was a big, barn-like building with picnic tables in it. The floor was concrete, the walls were wood with no insulation, and there was a big woodstove built out of a heavy metal drum.

With only twelve kids in our activity group, it was hard to avoid Jessica, but I tried. She was already there when I arrived with two guys from my cabin and I didn't look at her, so I didn't see her wave me over and I definitely didn't see the hurt look on her face.

Everyone sat around in little clusters talking and goofing off. Mr. George told us to "get cracking." Seriously – where do adults come up with these?

He left to get a cup of coffee, leaving us to get "underway." The teachers and counsellors aren't supposed to help with Talent Night, but some do. I watched Mr. George yawn and scratch his butt as he meandered out of the pavilion and decided that he was not going to be a big contributor to Talent Night.

One small cluster of kids, who appeared to actually be on topic, started to get loud and excited. I walked toward them.

One of the girls, Lacy, stood up on the picnic table and raised her voice above the echoing noise. "Hey you guys, we have an idea for a skit."

There were a few groans, a smattering of "whatevers," and a general quieting-down. Lacy explained the idea, which was a skit one of the kids had seen at her bible camp. It sounded funny, but it only had five or six characters in it and the rules required that everyone in the group had to participate. That rule was created to torture people like me.

A discussion started on how to cram extra people into the skit. Walk-ons? Human furniture? A choir, perhaps? The only thing worse than being in a skit is being crammed into a skit as an obvious extra. The theatrical equivalent of leftovers for dinner.

Dylan stood up on the bench of the picnic table

and addressed the muttering crowd. "We could do two skits. Maybe you guys who came up with that idea can get going on it and the rest of us could do another one," he said.

The first group moved away as Dylan outlined another skit to those who remained. It was about a family dinner, so we set up a table and gathered some chairs. The skit was corny but had potential because it ended with us throwing water at the audience. Also, since the whole skit was about people coming to the front door and interrupting dinner, we could keep thinking up doorbell people until we'd found a role for everyone in the group. I figured the people who came to the door would definitely have to speak, so in hopes of avoiding any lines, I hurried to the table and sat down. Maybe I could be the deaf-mute grandfather.

Jessica joined our group since all she would have to do in our skit was sit at the table, which she could do even with a bad leg.

She was sitting across from me, trying to catch my eye. When I did chance a peek at her, she looked glum. But she should have looked sorry – hand-wringing, blood-shot-eyes, haven't-slept-in-days sorry. And she didn't. So, I ignored her.

Dylan volunteered to be the father since he knew the lines and it was the father who kept getting up to answer the door. "Who's gonna be my wife?" he asked. He cocked an eyebrow and straightened his imaginary tie.

There was one of those laser-speed, non-verbal conversations that girls have and they apparently "decided" that Julia (a tall, dark, gorgeous girl from St. Joe's) would be the mother. Dylan grinned and winked at her. Me, I would have fainted.

Anyway, before I knew what was happening, I was the son and Dylan was telling me we'd "ad lib" a conversation to get the play going. Ad lib? Was he nuts? I needed a script in real life.

"So, how was your day, son?" Dylan asked in a corny, deep voice.

"I am fine, thank you father. How was your day?"

There was a one-second bubble of complete silence, then everyone burst out laughing. I looked at my hands and willed my cheeks to stop burning.

"A bit old fashioned there, Charles. Let's bring it into this century, okay? So how was your day, son?"

I looked at Dylan, hoping for a hint. He grinned at me.

"Um, it totally sucked, dude. And yours?"

The laughter was quieter this time. I thought I heard a hint of impatience in it.

"Why don't you actually say something about your day, okay Charles? Maybe say something about a math test. Oh, and don't ask about my day. Kids don't really care about their parent's day, do they? So…how was your day, son?"

I sighed and spoke in a flat voice. "I had a math test. It was hard. I – I probably failed. I might be failing math. I'm worried, Dad."

I looked up from my white knuckles gripping the edge of the table to sneak a look, as the snickers around me turned into groans. Dylan's face was unreadable. The kid with all the freckles slapped me on the back. "Jeez, Chuckie Cheese – first day with a family or what?"

I shot a dirty look at him, but in the process my eyes accidentally met Jessica's and the pity in them threw me over the edge.

I pushed my chair back and jumped up. The chair scraped loudly across the concrete floor and all the snickering and groaning stopped abruptly.

"I don't want to be in your lame skit," I said loudly. I started to walk toward the door.

"But everyone has to be in it," one of the girls whined.

"I'm the director," I snapped, without turning back. "And I'm on a break." I slammed the door behind me and marched across the field toward my cabin as fast as I could.

My throat had that aching, pre-cry feeling, so I started to run and once I started, I couldn't stop. I ran past the cabin and onto the trail that led down to the beach and when I got there, I saw a path that went behind the boathouse and into the woods to the south. I ran and ran until I didn't feel like crying anymore and I was too out of breath to be mad. And then I ran some more until even my embarrassment was too winded to care. When I couldn't go any further, I stopped, put my hands on my knees, and gasped for air.

Camp sucked.

I looked around. I'd gone a lot further than I intended. In fact, I was probably way outside camp boundaries. I peered into the trees and saw traces of colour. Not forest colours either, but a bright splotch of yellow. I started toward it without thinking. When I got close enough to see that it was a tent, I was also close enough to see that the guy coming out of it was my look-alike.

I dropped down into the bushes and watched the man's back disappear into the trees. I wasn't really aware of my feet moving, but before I'd even finished deciding what to do, I found myself standing in front of the tent with my eyes darting everywhere at once. I pushed up my glasses about 800 times as I stood there. Would unzipping a tent flap be considered a break-and-enter?

And then, I was in. It smelled funny and the floor of the tent was covered with dirty clothes, a balled-up sleeping bag, books, a water jug. If messes were art, this place was a masterpiece. Also, that weird tent-light thing was happening, so everything had a slightly unearthly glow (but a decidedly earthy aroma). Whoever he was, he wasn't on a weekend camping trip, he lived here. This was his life, at least for the present time, protecting these trees. Was he nuts? Or was there more to this "save the forest" thing than I'd thought? I had a tendency to tune out my mom, but now I was seeing the front line of the battle she was always talking about.

I wrinkled my nose to squint into the opposite corner. Out of the sea of chaos rose one little island – an upside-down milk crate with a few items arranged neatly on it: a shaving kit, a notebook and pen, a little black bag with a toothbrush sticking out of it, and a picture frame.

Well, seriously, who could resist that?

I shuffled across the tent on my knees and picked up the frame.

The photo was of a group of people arranged loosely in three rows, with the front row sitting cross-legged, the second kneeling, and the back row standing. Almost everyone looked like they were in their late teens or early twenties. It must have been a hot day because they were all in shorts and t-shirts. A few of the guys had their shirts off. Everyone's hair was either messy or tied back with a bandana or a ponytail. Many of them were barefoot. They were all so close together, they looked connected. Everyone had their arms draped over the shoulders of the person next to them. It was a photo of one squirmy, happy monster with twenty-one heads.

On the white border of the photo, someone had written, *Camp Douglas, 2005.*

I was born in 2006. My heart stopped and started up again with a painful thud.

And there was Mom! Right at the back, her right arm was around my large twin and his arm was around her. She was looking directly at the camera, her head back slightly. She looked like she was laughing at something someone had said. Shell wasn't looking at the camera, he was looking at Mom, leaning towards her slightly with a wide grin on his face.

I recognized this young version of Mom – I'd seen pictures – but there was a glow about her in this one that I'd never seen. She was standing with her weight on one leg, opposite hip jutting out, and she looked so … everything, so graceful and relaxed, strong and confident. So content.

I stared at the picture for ages. I'm not sure what I was trying to figure out, but I slowly became aware of feeling desperate to talk to her. This version of her that I held in my hands. Was she the same person I'd grown up with?

Why did looking at her joyful face make me happy and sad at the same time?

Then I studied Shell as though all the answers to my life might be hidden in his expression as he gazed at my mom. Did he love her? If he had known about me, my life might have been very different. How could they have been so clearly in love and not even exchanged information?

When a story is just a story, it's pretty easy to just accept it without question. But my story had just come to life, and so far, it was providing more questions than answers.

Before I realized what I was doing, I had the frame turned over and was slipping the photo out. How could I leave without the only evidence I'd ever had?

An image flashed into my mind: Shell reporting the theft to Mr. Garabaldi and The Ear doing a bunk-by-bunk search through the camp to see who'd been off site. I exhaled slowly and pushed the photo back into its place.

My hands were shaking and my stomach felt like I'd just done something horrid and now had to tell Mom.

Like the time I stole money from her purse and bought candy with it. I was sick for two days and it wasn't the candy's fault. I didn't feel better until I confessed everything. But I had returned the photo to the frame. Why did my stomach still feel so sick?

I put the picture exactly where it had been, knee-walked backwards, and re-zipped the tent flap behind me.

I went straight back the way I'd come, found the path, and walked quickly to the boathouse, where I started to run. Everyone was getting ready for the evening campfire when I arrived at the cabin. One of the guys from my activity group approached me with a look on his face that said, *what happened to you?* I cut him off before he could get started about the stupid skit.

I stuck to myself until lights out. In our bunks, the bedtime conversation carried on forever. Was it only last night I had been entertained by the jokes, insults, and farts criss-crossing the cabin? I lay there wishing they'd shut up and go to sleep because now that I knew what I knew ... well, I had to know more, didn't I?

It was licorice-black by the time the cabin fell quiet.

I counted to a thousand, just to be sure everyone was deeply asleep, and then inched my sleeping bag zipper down as slowly and quietly as I could. Note to self: next time, don't zip it up!

And go to bed with your clothes on, I thought as I groped around under my bunk for my jeans. I pulled my sweatshirt over my head and felt the tag scrape across my face. Standing in the pitch-black, I twisted the shirt around until the tag was in the back. I put my first shoe on the wrong foot, changed it, then couldn't find the second one. I got down carefully and began feeling around under the bunk. I was not excited about putting my hand too far under there. We cleaned the cabin ourselves and I can tell you for a fact, no one swept under the bunks. I was just starting to get freaked out imagining an army of spiders marching toward my fingers, when I knocked my water bottle over with a crash. I froze, my eyes bugging out, trying to find some light in the dark cabin. Over the buzz in my own ears, I heard a couple of guys grunt and roll over and then it was quiet again. I counted to three hundred and started moving again. My shoe was under the wrong bunk, naturally, but I found it eventually, reminding myself not to put my filthy hands on my face. I got up slowly, aware of the creaking boards in the old fir flooring. I took one tiny step at a time until I was at the door, then stood and breathed a few times. It is really easy to forget to breathe when you're terrified. Have you noticed that?

I opened that cabin door like a pro. I had practice from when Grandma brought cookies or cake to our house and I had to sneak out of my bedroom and past Mom sleeping in the front room to get to the kitchen.

Even when I was well away from the cabins, I kept my flashlight off, allowing my eyes to adjust to the dark. I took the route behind the nurse's cabin, figuring the protestors would all be at the firepit by now. As I picked my way through the bush, I tried not to think about what would happen if I got caught. I tried not to think of anything but stepping carefully.

When I got close to the clearing, I chose a spot to kneel down. Adjusting this way and that to give myself the best view of the fire circle, I almost didn't notice the big, dark shape creeping toward the clearing from another angle, off to my right and slightly behind me. I shoved my glasses up onto my nose and squinted into the night. It was Black Hoodie Guy, and he had no idea that I was there.

As he moved toward the circle, he was also moving closer to me. I crouched lower. I was trying to mentally shrink myself or possibly turn invisible. When he took a step around a tree, he veered slightly away from me and I exhaled a lungful of air. I stared into the dark to make sense of his weird shape. He was carrying something long and narrow like a baseball bat. No – it had two handles. Like big hedge clippers.

Strange time for trimming bushes.

He crept forward inches at a time now. It took him so long, my legs were getting cramped from crouching. He seemed to have a destination in mind and kept looking toward the clearing. Even if they'd heard him, I don't think anyone could have seen him– they would be looking out into total darkness.

He finally stopped a few feet from the edge of the clearing and I watched him flatten himself on the ground. What the heck?

He started to slither forward like a snake. I stood up slowly, well-hidden and increasingly curious. I strained my neck to push my head forward, still too scared to risk taking a step.

When he held up the hedge clippers, everything clicked into place in my head.

Not hedge clippers, but wire cutters. Big ones! The kind that go through heavy chains and metal fences.

Or guy wires holding tree platforms in place.

I could just make out the wire he was working on, but I couldn't tell which tree it was connected to.

I scanned the platforms, trying to see if anyone was up there, but I couldn't tell. My heart was pounding as I visualized someone plummeting to the ground.

"Hey! Hey!" I yelled, jumping up and down, waving my arms like windmills. All I could think to yell was more *Hey*s. Black Hoodie stood up and sprinted away in the general direction of the lake.

But now, all the people around the fire were looking my way and a few of them were coming toward me. Two of the guys plunged into the bush and ran at me, one of them turning on a flashlight as he ran, shining it into my face. I stuck my arms straight up, like the bad guy in a cop show. The bigger of the two grabbed me and said, "Come on."

He dragged me forward, steadying me as I stumbled along beside him in the dark, and pushed me into the circle of people standing around the fire.

"Why were you shouting, kid? And what were you doing out there in the first place?"

It was Shell. He stepped in front of me and my heart stopped with a bang as he studied my face. I swallowed.

"I saw a guy trying to cut that cable, so I yelled." I pointed to where the guy wire was anchored to the ground. One of the men went over and studied it with his light.

"Cut marks! Which way did he go, kid?"

I pointed, trying to keep my arm from trembling, and a handful of people hurried off into the woods.

I looked back at Shell, who was still studying my face.

"I'm Shell," he said. "Who are you?"

I cleared my throat. "My name's Charles," I said, but it came out a whisper. I cleared my throat again and waited.

"Where'd you come from?" he asked.

Interesting question, I thought.

"Camp Mingle," I said.

"Well, you better get back. You're not supposed to be here, are you?"

"No," I said, dropping my eyes and my volume. "Are you?"

His eyebrows shot up and he laughed. "Good point, kid. On second thought, why don't you stay and have a cup of tea with us? And you can tell us how you came to be hiding in the bushes at our camp."

And there I was – sitting at a campfire with my dad.

CHAPTER 10

You know, when I was seven or eight, I had tonsillitis. It wasn't so bad that I had to have my tonsils out, but it was bad enough that I had a wicked high fever. The kind that makes you delirious. Apparently, I walked out to the kitchen at one point and told Mom that the giraffe was going to crash the airplane if she didn't hurry up and do something! The fever went on for a day and a half and I slept for most of it. That sleep was filled with crazy dreams, like muskrats doing the vacuuming and me trying to drive a car with a blindfold on. But there were also dreams about my father. Afterwards, I could only remember bits and pieces, but again and again, I was doing things with my dad. I never saw his face – I don't think – but I knew it was him. And we knew each other, you know? We were comfortable as though we'd always known each other. And we were doing things I'd never done – horseback riding and mountain climbing. But never once in those dreams was I sitting by a campfire with my father beside me.

I didn't know this man. He was a stranger. It might be the worst feeling I've ever experienced.

"So, what brought you over here tonight, Charles?"

I bit my lip. "Well…"

There was crashing behind us and everyone turned toward the noise. The search party was back and between the two biggest guys was Black Hoodie with hood up and face down.

"This the guy?" asked the beefy dude, looking at me.

I nodded. I was just thinking that Black Hoodie seemed kind of small, when he spoke.

"Charles!"

Everyone looked at me. I pushed up my glasses and squinted at the face in the dark oval of the hoodie. Beefy Dude pulled the hood off and I could see a face clearly at last.

"Dylan!"

CHAPTER 11

A fine pickle, as my Grandpa would say: evidence of attempted sabotage, a captured saboteur, and me, clearly connected to the bad guy.

"Um…" I looked back at Shell and did not like the look on his face.

Dylan was nearly yanked off his feet and shoved onto the log beside me.

"Don't move a muscle," growled the big guy whose name was not Beefy Dude after all, but Gerry. The little circle of angry protestors shuffled away from the fire to discuss our fate. I turned to Dylan.

"What the hell?" I hissed.

"Why are they so mad? Touchy crowd. Let's get out of here while we can."

I stared at him. Did he really not know what had happened? Or was he a good actor? Whether he had done it or not, if we took off with the protestors still believing Dylan was trying to cut down a tree fort, they'd just trot over to Camp Mingle to identify us and we'd be in trouble in both camps. If we stayed and tried to persuade them that Dylan was innocent, maybe, just maybe, they'd let us go and we could sneak back before anyone else found out. Problem was, I wasn't sure if he *was* innocent.

"They think you were trying to cut one of those wires," I said, pointing.

"What?! Why would they think that?"

Because I sort of told them so, I thought glumly.

"They must've mixed you up with another guy wearing a black hoodie who actually did try to cut the wire. What are you doing here anyway?"

"I was on my way to the girls' can when I saw the glow of fire through the trees. What can I say? I'm a curious guy."

"The *girls'* can?"

Dylan reached into the long front pocket of his hoodie and pulled out a box of clear plastic food wrap.

I stared, trying to keep my face neutral.

"You'd get sent home for that, you know. Besides, someone already did that one."

"Yeah, but they didn't get caught. Yet." He turned over the box of wrap. My name was written across the bottom in black marker.

My mouth dropped open.

"Relax, it was just a joke." He grinned as he pulled the roll of wrap out of the box and threw the cardboard into the fire. "There you go," he said, as I watched my name go up in flames. "Truce?"

What was a joke? Framing me? Or pretending to frame me? Had he actually planned to do the prank or not? I knew what Jessica would say, but I was more confused than ever. But whatever he meant about the joke, it was small potatoes compared to the larger unanswered question. Was Dylan *the* Black Hoodie Guy?

And suddenly, out of nowhere, Mr. Staff popped into my mind. Do you remember the neighbour I told you about? Mr. Cranky-pants, converted to kindness with the clever use of warm cookies? Well, he was in my head all of a sudden and I thought about how Mom *started* giving him the benefit of the doubt before she knew why he was so crabby all the time. I didn't know if Dylan was as evil as Jessica thought. But I needed to get the heck out of here.

I turned to Shell. "This is not the guy I saw cutting the wire. It was a man, not a kid. A man who was also wearing a black hoodie."

I didn't like the way Shell was looking at me. My stomach dropped. My first face-to-face interaction with my father and he looked like he was about to tell me he was disappointed in me.

"Look," I said as calmly as I could. "We had this huge lecture about watching out for forest fires and I overreacted when I saw your fire. I came to make sure it wasn't a wildfire and I saw Black Hoodie Guy – not Dylan – and I yelled to stop him. That's all, I swear."

"Why do call him 'Black Hoodie *Guy*?'" Shell asked.

I blinked. "Um, because he's a guy. In a black hoodie?" I had no idea what he was asking.

Shell stared hard at me a moment longer, then turned to Dylan. "And you?"

"Same thing – except the part about the man. I didn't see anyone until you saw me. I was also coming to make sure this wasn't a forest fire."

"Please," I said. "We need to get back to our cabins before we're missed."

"Wait here," Shell said.

He and a few others moved away from us to talk. When they were done, four of the protestors turned on their headlamps and headed out into the bush again. Shell came back and stood in front of me and Dylan. "You can go. Stick together, keep your flashlights on, and go straight back. You hear me?"

We both nodded like dashboard bobbleheads. As we headed into the black woods, I couldn't help wondering how safe it was to send two kids into the forest in the middle of the night when you believed that a crazy guy was out there somewhere. Perhaps Shell was not "parent material," as Grandpa would say.

I forced myself to stop thinking about the wire-cutter because he might have been out there, somewhere in the dark, watching us. Or, worse, he might be walking right beside me. I opened my mouth to ask Dylan for the truth and shut it again. I didn't want to know. Not right now. I was too exhausted.

I concentrated on not losing my way, adjusting my course slightly toward the glow of the yard lights that stayed on all night in the main field of our camp. Without another word to Dylan, I stepped out of the bush and onto the grass and headed for my cabin.

CHAPTER 12

I woke up to Mr. George standing over my bunk, shouting, "Wake up!"

I grabbed my glasses and jammed them onto my face. The cabin door was open and the sun was shining outside. Every other bunk was empty.

"Why are you yelling?" I sputtered.

"Because this is the fifth time I've tried to get you up. You're late for breakfast, and more to the point, *I* am late for breakfast. If you want to eat, you better move." He walked out the door.

Did I want to eat? I got up and stretched. Yup – starving.

I was dressed and halfway to the dining hall before I remembered I was supposed to be mad at Jessica. This was no time to be without a best friend, I decided.

As soon as I walked in, I saw her. She was sitting in the back corner again, waving cautiously at me. I could almost hear the telepathic apology she was sending me. I waved and the worried look on her face dissolved into a huge smile. She waved back like we hadn't seen each other in years and pointed to the chair next to her.

I got a plate of vaguely tomato-y French toast and joined her.

"Hey," she grinned. "I'm sorry about everything."

"Hey," I grinned back. It was surprisingly easy to forgive someone who was sorry. "It's okay. How's your ankle?"

"A little better."

Even though I was dying to catch her up on everything that had happened, I was also hungry like the hippo. I jammed some French toast into my mouth and chewed. I swallowed, leaned over to Jessica, and whispered, "He's my dad. For sure."

For the first time since I'd known her, Jessica was speechless. She was blinking at me like an owl and I could see the questions lining up in her head. Once she got her mouth working again, there'd be no stopping her. I held up my left hand like a stop sign while I shovelled down my breakfast with my right hand. I finished, tossed back half a glass of hippie apple juice, and stood up.

"C'mon, let's play some chess."

Moments later, I stood in the middle of the chess board, staring at the pieces without seeing them. "Give me a minute," I said to Jessica, who sat on the bench beside the board, ready to burst.

"Okay, let's see," I began. "Last night, after I left the skit fiasco – let me finish." Her mouth had already opened. She closed it.

"I went for a walk. Well, a run, actually, but it doesn't matter. I ended up in the woods behind the boathouse and saw Shell coming out of a tent. After he left, I snuck in and found a picture of my mom and him – hang on!" I said, as Jessica's mouth opened again.

"So, after everyone went to sleep, I went back to their camp again – seriously, Jessica, just shut it and let me finish, will you?

She closed her mouth again and nodded.

"I went back so I could learn more – to listen to their conversation. But then Black Hoodie Guy showed up." There was a tiny gasp but no interruption. I continued.

"He didn't see me and he crawled up to a guy wire – did I tell you about the platforms up in the trees?" She nodded, biting her lip.

"Anyway, he started cutting one of the wires with a big pair of wire cutters. I just reacted, you know? It was serious; someone could have gotten hurt. I jumped up and started yelling and Black Hoodie ran away, but they grabbed me and there I was, face-to-face with my dad." I stopped talking and looked at Jessica. Her eyes were huge, but she had stopped fidgeting.

"My dad," I said again, just to hear it, and continued. "Well, he was ticked off – wanted to know what I was doing there. I told him we'd had a big lecture on forest fires here at camp and that I saw their fire through the trees on the way to the bathroom and came to check it out."

Jessica forgot to be quiet. "He bought that?" she asked.

"I don't know. I don't think so, but once I told them about Black Hoodie Guy, they had more important things to worry about."

"They believed you about Hoodie?"

"Yes. They found the cut marks on the wire. So,

they charged off to find him while I stayed with … my dad. They came back shortly with a guy wearing a black hoodie. Guess who?" I was starting to enjoy myself now. It was a good story.

"Who?" Jessica jumped off the bench, yelling as she landed on the temporarily forgotten sprain before sitting back down with a thump. "Who?" she asked again through gritted teeth.

I waited a second for dramatic effect.

"Dylan!"

"Holy cow!" she shouted.

"Shhh!" I looked around, but no one was anywhere near us.

"Holy cow," she whisper-shouted. "I knew it, I knew it! That guy is pure evil. He – "

"Hold up, Jessica," I interrupted. "Dylan isn't Black Hoodie Guy. They nabbed the wrong black hoodie … guy." Why did Jessica's certainty about Dylan make me want to defend him?

Jessica's face was flushed. "Oh. My. Goddess. Are you kidding me? He gets caught red-handed right in front of you and you *still* want to stick up for him?"

"Okay, stop." I held up both hands in front of Jessica. "Don't talk," I said. I sat down beside her and she turned to face me. Her expression was somewhere between *Convince Me* and *You're Being an Idiot.*

"Look," I said. "I know you have decided that Dylan is the devil, but I'm not so sure. Either way, he is not the Black Hoodie Guy. That was a man. Dylan is a kid." Who was I trying to convince, Jessica or myself?

"How do you *know* it was a man and not a boy? You've only seen this guy – if it is a different guy – in the dark or from a long distance away. Or both. You've never stood close enough to him to compare his size with yours. You saw a scary-looking dude and your brain told you it must be a man. This is like first grade when you told everyone you saw Santa's sleigh flying through the air. It was Christmas Eve, you believed the story about Rudolph and his red nose, so when you saw a blinking red light in the night sky, your brain told you it was Santa's sleigh and that's what you saw. No one could convince you it was an airplane. This is the same thing."

I could feel how red my face was. "Okay, Professor, take it easy," I growled at her.

Jessica's theories were annoying; they were usually embarrassing in some way, and worse, they were often right.

It was true that I'd only ever seen Hoodie at night or from a long way off. And how likely is it that two guys wearing black hoodies would be running around the same patch of forest on the same night?

"But it doesn't make any sense, Jessica. Why would Dylan want to sabotage a protest camp? And what about the old car we found? We saw the hoodie there. Are you suggesting Dylan has a second home in a rusted-out wreck?"

"Well, who knows? Everyone loves a fort, right? But even if there are two different guys, I'm saying last night it had to have been Dylan. Seriously, Chuck, one

Black Hoodie Guy runs into the woods, gets chased, and another one is brought back a few minutes later? What are the chances of that?"

I shoved my sliding glasses back up my nose. Yes, what were the chances?

The bell gonged for the start of our first activity block.

"Are you coming to the ropes course to watch?" I asked Jessica.

"No. Mr. George said I could go to archery with another group. Might as well *do* something, right? But watch yourself, Chuck. Don't get anywhere near Dylan. Promise me!"

"Okay," I said and watched her stump off toward the archery range.

I sat down on the bench. Who'd have thought telling the story to Jessica would make it more confusing than it already was? I now had more questions than answers. Was Dylan the guy I'd seen sneaking around? Had he tried to cut the wire? And even if it wasn't him, why was he out there last night? The questions rolled around in my head.

There was one good thing about the black hoodie mystery, though; it distracted me from the question that made my stomach flip like a flapjack.

Had Shell recognized himself in my face?

CHAPTER 13

I was a few minutes late to the ropes course, but even so, I wasn't the last to arrive. I noticed right away that Dylan wasn't there. So did everyone else.

"Hey, where's Dylan?" someone asked.

One of his cabinmates replied. "He's still in bed; he's sick."

I was a bit disappointed because I had decided that I was going to keep a close eye on Dylan – without getting too close, since I'd promised Jessica I wouldn't. However, since he was a no-show, I turned my full attention to the activity.

Because the ropes require a lot of focus, for the next couple of hours I barely thought about my problems. I improved my social standing a bit by being one of only three campers who did the low ropes perfectly and was allowed to move on to the high ropes. The high ropes course *really* requires concentration, so I had to push all the interference out of my head. By the time we were finished, I felt better. Clearer.

It's not that I suddenly knew the answers to my questions, but I knew a couple of things. First, I knew that I couldn't let Jessica influence me so much. She might be right about Dylan, but she was always quick

to decide people were evil when she came to that deciding place. I'd seen her do it plenty of times. Personally,
I think it's because of her three older brothers. They
were always teasing her when she was little. They lied
to her when she was too young to know they were lying.
I think they teased the trust right out of her.

When I woke up that morning, I'd been fairly sure
that there were two black hoodie guys, and in five minutes, Jessica had me doubting myself again.

As for my other big question, I replayed my interaction with Shell and remembered him looking at me
strangely. Not the kind of strange you'd expect when
you find a kid hollering in the woods, more like the
kind of strange you feel when you meet someone for
the first time and they look familiar.

I avoided the dining hall altogether and foraged
my lunch from the fruit bowl in the front entrance of
the main hall.

I headed to the beach. The morning had been
partly cloudy, but now the sky was clearing and the
sun was revving up her engine.

I munched an apple and tried to clear my mind.
Or at least to free it from Jessica's theories. I needed
someone else in my head – someone who was good at
figuring stuff out. I pictured the Grands in their kitchen:
Grandpa and I would be sitting at the table drinking
hot chocolate and eating cookies. Grandpa would say
something like, *Lay all the pieces of the puzzle out in front
of you and figure out what you're missing. Then go after the
pieces you still need. They may be easier to find than you think.*

Grandma's mug would be getting cold as she jumped up to fill ours, refill the cookie plate, and stir something on the stove. If I could get her to sit still long enough, she'd probably want to know why I was trying to deal with all this alone when my best friend was here at camp with me.

Two heads are better than one, Cedar, my imaginary mom chimed in.

"It's Charles," I muttered under my breath. Mom was butting into my imagination uninvited – again – but she and imaginary Grandma were right. It was always easier to figure things out when Jessica and I did it together. I just needed to keep Jessica from getting carried away. I jumped up and ran back to the dining hall to get her.

Once she was settled on the bench by the chess board, I told her what Grandpa had said. Or would have. Or might have. You know what I mean.

"But just the facts, Jessica. Just what we know for sure. No opinions on anything. Especially Dylan. Agreed?"

"Right. Facts. Gotcha." Jessica nodded enthusiastically. "We know that someone is living in the abandoned car and they own a black hoodie. That's fact number one."

I nodded. "And number two is that someone is sneaking around the protestors' camp and they tried to cut the guy wire, which is serious. They also own a black hoodie."

"Check," said Jessica. "The third is that one of the

protestors is Shell and we are fairly certain that Shell is your dad."

She chewed her lip. "Maybe that's an opinion?"

"It's as close to fact as we're going to get without a blood test. What else do we know?"

Jessica continued. "Number four is that Dylan has a black hoodie and was caught in the woods by the protestors on the night of the attempted wire-cutting."

"Number five, so was I," I said quietly.

We both thought about that for a minute. I was wondering if Shell saw any difference between Dylan and me – just a couple of kids from Camp Mingle snooping around. Or did he see me differently?

I blinked. Not a fact.

"Okay, do we know motivation?" I asked. "I was in the woods to find out more about…Shell. Shell was in the woods to stop the logging company from clear-cutting the forest. We don't know why Dylan was there and we don't know why the other Black Hoodie Guy was there – if it is a different guy."

"So, the missing piece so far is the motivation of Black Hoodie Guy," Jessica said.

"Or *guys*," I said. "You and your crutches can't hide in the woods, so I'll go back this afternoon and find out what the protestors are saying about last night." And about the kid who looks like Shell, I thought. "Why don't you work on trying to figure out why Dylan was out last night? And whether he is the tenant of the car-condo?"

"Car-condo! Good one, Chuckie," snorted Jessica.

I let it go. You can only deal with so many things at a time.

It was free-choice afternoon, so we had our pick of almost any activity we wanted. Jessica decided to do whatever Dylan was doing, assuming he was feeling better, in order to see what she could find out.

I went to swimming. It had gotten quite hot already and there were tons of kids on the beach by the time I arrived. It would be easy to slip away unnoticed from this crowd. Easier still because the two lifeguards clearly had a thing for each other and were spending ninety-five percent of their attention on each other.

Another benefit of being a scrawny nobody: sneaking away without being noticed. It was practically my superpower.

I eased through the woods carefully since there were plenty of people out and about in both camps. I skirted around the tents and came up to the fire circle one tree at a time. But apparently the fire was not the meeting place in the daytime – only a couple of voices drifted to my hiding spot, and neither one was Shell's.

I decided to keep going toward the road. It made sense that they'd be at the road during the day; this was a blockade, right?

I stayed hunched down as I looked ahead, planning my route to the road. That was when I saw him. Ahead of me and off to my right, Black Hoodie Guy was creeping through the bush toward the road.

I dashed up to the next tree, watching Black Hoodie the whole time. We both moved tree to tree. He was unaware of my presence and moved forward as cautiously as I did. Before long, I could hear voices.

Hoodie had chosen a spot close enough that he could see and hear the little group of protestors on the road. He turned to settle against the tree he was hiding behind.

As he turned, I dropped into the bushes and peeked through the leaves. I pushed up my glasses to be sure.

It was Dylan.

Dylan *was* Black Hoodie Guy. Jessica had been right all along. Whatever he was up to, I didn't want to be part of it. I certainly didn't want to be blamed for it. I turned around and crawled away on my belly. When I thought it was safe, I got up and picked my way back through the trees.

I slowed as I went, not excited about having to listen to Jessica gloat. This was turning into a mess and trying to sort through it was giving me a headache. And, of course, there was the niggling worry that Dylan was up to something dangerous and I had left without warning anyone. On second thought, they could take care of themselves; they were adults and he was just a kid, after all.

As I walked, random thoughts ran through my mind: Dylan, the abandoned car, the black hoodie, the wires, Shell. It was too much. I arrived at the edge of the field and checked around to make sure no one saw me step out of the trees. Alone, I walked to my cabin.

By the time I was finally stretched out on my sleeping bag staring at the graffiti on the bottom of the bunk over my head, I could feel how tired I was from last night's adventure. I read a few of the knock-knock jokes scribbled in marker above me and thought sleepily about correcting the spelling.

I woke to the sound of the supper gong, feeling refreshed in spite of my dream about being chased by giant archery bows that were taller than me.

When I got to the dining hall, Jessica was already there. "Did you go back?" she asked. "What happened? Did you see Shell? Did you talk to him? What did you find out? I didn't find out anything. Dylan was nowhere to be found all afternoon." She stood up, balancing on one leg, and surveyed the dining hall. "Still not here," she said. "Weird." She shoved a spoonful of sloppy joe into her mouth and looked at me. "So?" she mumbled through greasy hamburger.

I watched her chew. "I saw Dylan over at the camp again. Spying on them. I took off before he saw me. I'm not going back again. Whatever he's up to, I don't want to get messed up in it." Now that I was saying it out loud, I realized how disappointed I was to know that I wouldn't see Shell again. I glanced at Jessica who looked like she might explode with the effort of not saying, *I told you so.*

I concentrated on my food while she chewed on the information I'd shared. And her sloppy joe.

"So, how do you feel? Knowing you won't see your dad again?" she asked carefully.

"Crappy."

She nodded and took another bite.

"But also, relieved," I said, surprising myself a little. "Is that nuts?" I asked.

"No, I get it."

She nodded toward a huddle of adults at the front of the hall. The Ear, one of the teachers from St. Joe's, and one of the camp counsellors. "What do you think *that's* about?" she asked.

I stood up and took another good look around the dining hall. Dylan still wasn't back and obviously the adults had finally noticed they were missing a kid. "Dylan," I said to Jessica. "He's still over there spying." I watched the huddle a while longer, and slowly, it dawned on me that I could end up in trouble, too. "Oh crap."

"What?" asked Jessica.

"If they go looking for him and talk to anyone at the camp, they'll hear about the Scrawny Kid. And that would be my second offence – that they know about – and I'll be sent home. What am I going to do?"

"Well, you could go over there and get him yourself. We could tell The Ear something to buy you some time."

"What can we tell him?" I was starting to panic. My brain gets sluggish when I panic.

Jessica struggled out of her chair and looked around the dining room. She plopped down again. "The nurse isn't here. Neither is Kevin. I heard he tripped running down the dock in his bathing suit and skinned his belly and arms. She's probably pulling splinters out of his forehead as we speak. Anyhow, we can tell The Ear that Dylan is sick. That we walked him up to the nurse's cabin and forgot to tell his counsellor. Oops. Very sorry. Our bad. By the time the nurse shows up without him, you'll both be back. But you better get going. I'll go talk to The Ear."

"Okay," I said. I had no time to think it through. Jessica was already heading toward the cluster of adults. I quickly slipped out the back door and headed for the woods.

Halfway to the protest camp, I realized I wasn't wearing a jacket and the wind was picking up. Charcoal clouds had rolled in over the last hour and it was like dusk already. Dylan was not going to be sitting behind the same tree where I last saw him several hours ago and I had no idea where to look for him. I stopped in my tracks.

What was I thinking? If Dylan was up to something, I was going to get myself blamed as an accomplice. This was far bigger than just trying to keep my name out of a conversation between the two camps. I had to get out of here.

I turned around and ran smack into Shell.

CHAPTER 14

I was sitting alone on a log by the protesters' fire.

Again.

Shell and Gerry and several others were having a conference about the information I had just provided: a kid was missing from our camp and the last time I saw him, it was here. Shell came and sat beside me. He ran his fingers through his hair and looked at me. "And what were you doing here when you saw him?" he asked.

"I'm just curious. About protests and stuff," I mumbled. "Have you seen Dylan?"

"No." It felt like he was considering saying more, so I sat still and waited.

"I'm sure he's fine, but there has been someone else around, as you know." He looked at me more closely. "You haven't seen that guy, have you?"

What was I going to say? *Oh that. Turns out it was the kid all along. There was no other guy. Sorry about that.*

"Nope."

Gerry walked over and gestured to Shell. They talked quietly again and Shell came back to the fire. I was shaking. Maybe from cold or maybe from being in a big fat hairy mess that I made for myself and didn't know how to fix. It was dark now, like the sun had already gone down although it was just early evening. And it was starting to rain.

Shell took his jacket off and handed it to me. My dad was giving me his jacket.

As I put it on, that old car came back into my head again. It was the only hiding place I knew of and I wanted to help. Was I worried about Dylan? Did I want my dad to think I was a good guy? Who knows?

I told Shell about that first day of camp when Jessica and I had found the wreck of the car and the black hoodie inside it and the other things we'd found there. Shell listened carefully without interrupting.

"Do you think you could find that car again?" Shell asked.

I didn't know if I could in the dark, but I was pretty good at maps and directions, so I closed my eyes and tried to picture the area from an overhead view: our camp, their camp, the trail we used the day we found the car ... I thought I could do it.

"I think I can get you to the right area. If we spread out, we can probably find it," I said with uncharacter-istic confidence.

The group was organized in a few minutes with Shell and me in the lead, and we headed away from the warmth and light of the fire into the cold, dark shadows. Flashlights and headlamps appeared out of pockets and backpacks as the group fanned out. It took only a few steps for the confidence to start wiggling out of my shoulders and down my trembling arms.

Walking in the forest can be disorienting, especially without sunlight. Straight lines don't exist no matter how hard you wish for them. I was fairly sure we needed to go straight northwest toward the lake and somehow we circled around and headed back toward Camp Mingle. I stared at the dark sky, hoping for a clue. I made my best guess and we corrected the angle and continued. I was cold, miserable, and scared. How had I gotten myself into this?

We trudged on as the night grew darker and chillier. I was so tired, all I could think about was my bed. Or even my sleeping bag on a plywood cot.

Finally, the guy on the end of the line called out, "Over here!" We'd almost missed it.

A dozen flashlights investigated the car corpse. The protestors knew immediately who had been living there from the things they pulled out to examine. He'd obviously "moved out" in a hurry and had left a lot of his stuff behind. The guy's name was Guy. You know – the guy who was trying to cut the guy wire. (I can hear you yelling *As if!* but it's the truth.)

Shell dragged something heavy out from under a pile of cardboard and held it up in the flood of headlamp beams: wire cutters.

Over all the chatter and the wind, I thought I heard a shout. I moved a step away from the crowd to listen, and it happened again. This time it was louder and the others heard it as well. We all turned in the direction of the sound.

Suddenly, a dazzling light was shining right in my eyes and I couldn't see a thing. It was much brighter than a headlamp or a flashlight and I covered my face. There was mass confusion; I could hear people yelling and stumbling around.

"Everyone stand still," the first voice yelled over the noise, and we did. "I've got the kid."

I shielded my eyes with my arm and squinted toward the voice. A slouching shape stood holding a smaller one by the hood of his jacket. It had to be Dylan.

Normally, I'm the type to panic in these situations and then have to get out of it using oatmeal for brains because mine have turned to mush. But not tonight. My brain jumped into gear. Maybe it was the cold or my fatigue, I don't know, but as my Grandpa would say, I'd reached the end of my rope and it was time to tie a knot. I cleared my throat.

"Turn out the light for a second so we can see if you have the kid," I shouted in my loudest – and lowest – voice. The spotlight flicked off for a second, and when it did, I dropped to the ground. The light came back on and I held my breath, but he didn't notice that I'd disappeared. I inched forward as quietly as I could, heading to my right, to slowly circle around behind Black Hoodie Guy. Well, just Guy.

Shell started talking to Guy, asking him why he tried to cut the wire.

"I told you idiots a million times, the only way to get the public on our side is to do a little damage and blame the logging company."

"And we told you a million times that's not what we're about. It's not why we're here. And what are you going to do now, Guy? On top of everything else, you're going to add kidnapping? Just let the kid go before you get in over your head. We'll forget the wire-cutting if you let him go."

"Sure you will. No sir, he's my ticket out. I'm leaving and the kid's coming for safe passage. If anybody follows us, the kid is going to feel some pain. Let me go and I'll leave him somewhere safe."

Call me crazy, but somewhere in my head I thought I could still fix all this without getting into trouble: save Dylan, make a deal with the protesters, sneak back into camp, crawl into my sleeping bag, and pretend nothing had happened tonight. Maybe I could even forget about meeting my dad. My mom calls this my "tendency to retreat from the truth."

Once I was behind Guy and Dylan, I stopped crawling. I couldn't go any further without being heard. I felt around me carefully and soon my hand wrapped around the tip of a fallen alder tree. The end I was touching was raised a few inches off the ground. If I was lucky, I might be able to move this end and have the other end make enough noise to distract Guy for a second. Then what? I sent a Luke Skywalker Jedi message to my Darth Vader dad: *Jump him when he's distracted. And may the Force be with you.*

I groped around with my left hand until I found a short, thick stick, good for throwing. I got to my feet carefully, found the end of the alder, and prepared to stomp on it. At the same time, I would throw the stick as far as I could to my left. I stood frozen like that while Shell continued to try to reason with Guy, but it wasn't going anywhere and I could hear Guy's voice getting more agitated. It was now or never, or he might do something stupid. Dylan could get hurt.

I yelled my best war cry, threw the stick as far as I could, and stomped down on that alder with every ounce of my scrawny strength. The other end of the alder rose up and hit the ground with a whump like heavy artillery at the same moment the stick skittered loudly across the top of the salal, twenty feet away in the opposite direction. And the second I yelled, Shell yelled too.

Guy whipped around toward the thump of the alder, back the other way toward the stick, then toward me. Shell was already charging forward, so Guy swung back toward him. It was just enough time. I lunged forward and wrapped my scrawny arms around Guy's legs, nailing him at full speed. He let go of Dylan as he hit the ground – and he hit it hard enough to wind himself, thank you very much. Shell arrived in time to sit on Guy's chest, pinning his arms at his sides.

I stood up, chest heaving. From his seat on Guy, Shell gave me a high five. "Good job, kid!" I nodded happily, too out of breath to speak.

Shell got off of Guy and two of the bigger men yanked him up and dragged him away. That was when I finally noticed Dylan staring at me.

"What are you looking at?" I asked. Now that the action-hero adrenalin was draining out of my body, I felt tired, weak, and shaky. And far too cranky to deal with Dylan. Or a dad who didn't know he was one.

Actually, the inside of me felt as weak as the outside all of a sudden and I wanted to go bury my head under my pillow and forget this day – this week – had happened at all.

I turned to Shell. "I don't know what happens next, but I'm hoping it doesn't include me. Ever. I'd like to go back to camp and go to bed, you know what I mean?"

"Me too," squeaked Dylan.

Shell tilted his head and studied us. "Come back to the fire and we'll talk it over."

Would this night never end?

I don't know what they did with Guy, but he wasn't at the fire circle. Shell didn't want to talk to us, he just wanted to make sure he wasn't sending injured children into the woods. He looked us both over and agreed to leave us out of the official version of the story, whatever that was.

"You did good, kid," he said and clapped me on the back. Gerry shone his light from my face to Shell's.

"Jeez, Shell! It's uncanny when you stand right beside him like that!" I blushed from my hairline to my chin. Perhaps this was my moment. I looked at Shell and he was studying me closely.

I chickened out. I turned and started walking away.

"Hey kid, wait up. I'll walk you to the camp boundary," said Gerry, aiming his flashlight beam in front of me.

"Suit yourself," I muttered and kept going. I could hear Dylan stumbling along as well, but I stomped through the bush without looking back.

Once it was just the two of us and we could see the camp lights in the distance, Dylan started yapping at me about getting our stories straight. I ignored him at first, but finally I whirled around and hissed at him, "What were you doing over there?"

Dylan stared straight ahead for a second, then began to speak in a shaky voice. "I was looking for someone. I thought my brother might be there."

"Tell the truth, you jerk!"

"That is the truth," he snapped. His face scrunched up like he was trying not to cry, then suddenly the words tumbled out of him. His brother, Ben, had run away from home two years ago.

Their foster home.

Dylan had received postcards from him the first year that described a logging protest group. He talked about setting up camps to block logging operations that used clear-cutting. Then Dylan's foster family moved and he didn't get any more postcards. When he saw the protest camp as he arrived, he decided to come see if Ben might be here. Or if anyone in the camp knew him.

"Why didn't you just ask the camp people to let you come over and ask? What's with all the sneaking?"

Dylan rolled his eyes at me. "You should talk. Obviously, we both wanted to keep what we were doing a secret. None of my friends at this school know that I'm a foster kid."

I took a real close look at Dylan.

He was telling the truth.

"What about you?" he asked. "Why were you there?"

He was looking at me strangely. Did he already know the answer?

Moment of truth. Could I trust him or not? I could almost hear Jessica screaming, *Are you nuts, Chuck?*

"I was looking for someone too," I said. "It's too complicated to explain right now."

He seemed to study my face for a second. I knew he wanted to press for more, but instead he just nodded. "Okay," he said.

We walked the rest of the way back in silence and went our separate ways at the field.

When I got to my cabin and found it dark and quiet, I nearly laughed with relief.

I tiptoed past all the lumps in bunks and crawled into my sleeping bag. Almost immediately, I heard footsteps approaching the cabin. The door opened and I recognized Mr. George's silhouette in the door.

Crap.

He stepped softly across the cabin and knelt down beside me.

"You hurt?" he asked.

"No."

"You sick?"

"No."

He grunted. "Go to sleep. The director will see you right after breakfast."

CHAPTER 15

"Are you sure about this?" I asked. I pushed up my glasses and squinted at Jessica.

"I'm sure," she said.

We were sitting on a bench near the parking lot, waiting to be picked up. I had a big lump of dread in my belly. It felt like I'd swallowed a snow boot.

Although I was the one being sent home, Jessica had chosen to leave with me. When I'd gone to tell her the story behind why I was being kicked out of camp, she was stunned into silence for a minute, then started talking about the injustice of it all and after a while I tuned her out.

"It's no fun on crutches anyway," she concluded. "Besides, you're gonna need backup."

Actually, I was glad she was coming. Her presence would spare me a two-hour lecture in the car. I contemplated inviting her for a sleepover. Maybe she'd like to stay until I turned eighteen and moved out.

My mom doesn't have a car. Since the moment the director told me that someone would be here to pick me up at ten am, I'd been running a repeating loop-prayer: *Please let it be Grandpa, please let it be Grandpa.* Under normal circumstances, I would be hoping for

Mom – Grandpa could actually be quite tough on me when I screwed up and I knew how to handle Mom, if you know what I mean. But I didn't want to deal with her right now because of the Shell thing. I didn't even want to see her.

Jessica rested her bad ankle on top of her suitcase which I'd hauled over here after two trips with my own gear. The camp provided no assistance for those sent home in shame.

My morning had started with mild nausea followed by a staring contest with my breakfast, followed by more nausea. I almost heaved in the director's office. It had been a whirlwind morning after a crappy sleep and I was already tired before I had to haul all our stuff up here.

Jessica nudged an ant with the tip of her crutch. "Can I ask you a question, Chuck?" She'd been uncharacteristically cautious with me all morning. Like she was worried I might blow a gasket.

"Sure," I said without looking at her. The nausea stayed under control if I didn't move at all. Not even my head.

"Why didn't you tell the director the part about saving the tree people? Maybe being a hero would have cancelled out being off the grounds."

I sighed. "Because the director would have told my mom I was at the protest camp and I don't want her to know. Not yet, anyhow."

The snow boot in my belly kicked.

Jessica nodded. "Oh."

We were quiet again and I focussed my attention on a pair of ravens hopping around the parking lot.

"So, Chuck," Jessica started hesitantly.

"Hm?"

"Are you ever going to meet him now? Did you get his last name?"

Crap. That would have been a good idea. "It's not that I never want to, it's just that I need to think about it. It was one thing to see him, but it's a whole other thing to meet him as his son."

"Good point," Jessica said. "Plus, there's the whole thing with your mom. Wow."

"What do you mean?" The belly boot shifted uncomfortably.

"Well, it's going to be big for her too. She thought this guy was gone forever and now he's back. Maybe she's still in love with him. Or maybe she'll be freaked out about sharing you with someone else. Or..."

"Stop!" I cut her off before I up-chucked the boot. "You need to stop."

"Sorry," she said.

I hadn't even thought about how this would be for Mom. What if she got all hippie-woo-woo on me? What if she took one look at Shell and moved us straight into the nearest treehouse? What if he was an idiot?

But what if he wasn't? What if I could have a family like everyone else, a dad to visit over the summer holidays and double the Christmas presents?

"What are you thinking?" Jessica asked.

Before I could answer, Grandpa's car pulled into the

parking lot. So far, so good. I squinted into the car to see who was behind the wheel.

Mom.

Double crap. I picked up Jessica's suitcase while Mom walked over to us. She gave Jessica a tight little smile.

"Hello, Jess."

"Hi, Ms. Dance. Did my mom give you the letter?" Jessica asked her.

"I have your release papers right here."

Jessica sighed with relief. The director said she would not be leaving without a signed letter from a parent and getting anything accomplished quickly at her house was a minor miracle.

"I have to go see the director, then we'll go." Mom walked away. She hadn't even looked at me.

I loaded the car while Jessica watched.

"We're leaving, Chuck. Your dad's right there, now. But in a week, he could be gone and you'll never find him again. Aren't you worried?"

Thanks to Dylan's arrival at that moment, I pushed it out of my mind once more.

Dylan dropped his backpack, sleeping bag, and suitcase in the grass at the edge of the parking lot.

"Are your ... folks coming?" I asked.

He nodded glumly, pointing to a blue car roaring down the lane toward us. It stopped in a cloud of dust and a big man got out. He looked like he'd gotten up too early and wasn't happy about it.

"Were you trying to run away?" he barked at Dylan.

"No, I wasn't. I swear," Dylan said, his face blazing.

"Get in the car," the man said to Dylan.

I turned and walked over to Dylan as he pushed his suitcase into the backseat. I stuck out my hand and looked Dylan in the eye. "Thanks for coming to look for me, Dylan," I said loudly. I checked to make sure the man was listening.

Dylan shook my hand, raising his eyes to meet mine. I thought I saw a glint of gratitude there and his shoulders straightened slightly with that familiar Dylan confidence.

"Bye," I said and walked away as he climbed into the backseat. Jessica and I watched the car roar away.

"Wow. That was one cranky dad," Jessica said.

"Foster dad," I said.

"Oh," she said quietly. I could see by her face that she was rearranging things in her head. Her face softened.

We climbed into the backseat of Grandpa's car and waited.

Mom got into the car and started it without saying a word.

I stared out the window, thinking that maybe it was all for the best. As the miles slipped by, it was getting easier to breathe. Maybe this whole thing was just meant to be a chance to see my dad. To know that he's out there. To know that he's dedicated to the environment. That's a good thing, right?

As we detoured around the protest camp, I saw Mom looking into the trees. Was she thinking about her own protest days? If she hadn't become pregnant, would she still be living in camps, trying to protect the forest? I studied the back of her head and resolved to start paying better attention to her rants about the environment.

I watched all the trees ticking by the window and wondered what the Grands would think of all this. I imagined myself telling them this story one day, but no matter how I played it in my head, eventually Grandpa was going to say, *Why didn't you say anything, boy?*

I chewed the inside of my cheek and played with my hair. I never should have invited the Grands into my brain. I could see Grandma fidgeting with her sweater and looking worried, and I knew perfectly well what she would say: *Your mother has a right to know you met Shell.*

That didn't feel too good. Maybe I should just tell her now. With Jessica here, Mom probably wouldn't freak out completely. I turned over the pros and cons for a couple of silent, sickening miles. Then I pushed the argument out of my head and went for it.

"Mom, I have something big to tell you, so you better pull over."

And I told her everything. She was hanging on to the back of the front seat, turned around so she was facing me, and there were times in the story where her hands were gripping the headrest like she was trying to choke it to death. Her face was the whitest I've ever seen it and even after I finished, she didn't say a word; she just stared at me with huge, unblinking eyes.

It didn't appear that she was going to speak anytime soon, so I kept going. "I don't know if I want to see him again or not, but I thought you should know." I looked at my hands. "In case you want to see him," I mumbled. I had no idea what she was thinking or feeling, and it was starting to weird me out a little.

"Are you okay, Mom?"

"Yes, Cedar, I'm okay, but I need a moment. I'm going to take a walk. Will you two be okay here?"

I could only nod, but Jessica reassured Mom that we'd be fine and she should go ahead and take her time.

"What do you think she's thinking?" I asked Jessica. "If it's too late to put me up for adoption?"

Jessica let out a gasp of laughter as though she'd been holding her breath. "Atta boy, Chuck. Don't lose your sense of humour. Let's see … she's probably thinking about whether she wants to see him again."

I grunted.

"But mostly," she continued, "I'll bet she's wondering how to handle it if you want to get to know him." She was quiet for a moment. "Maybe she's worried that you'll like Shell better than her or have more in common with him. Let's face it, you and your mom don't share a lot of common ground." She looked out the window toward my mom, pacing along the road's shoulder. "I bet she's scared."

"I don't even know if I want to know him," I muttered. As soon as I said it, I knew it wasn't true. You can tell yourself all sorts of nonsense in your head, but when you say it out loud, it's a whole different thing. And judging by the look on Jessica's face, she wasn't buying it either.

"I want to go back," I blurted. "Before he leaves. Today. Just in case. I don't want to lose track of him." I felt excited as I spoke, as though the snow boot in my stomach had turned into a butterfly.

"You should go talk to your mom privately. I'll wait here. Go on."

"Okay. Thanks, Jessica," I said.

"It's Jess, butthead," she grinned.

I caught up with Mom easily. She heard me coming and turned. There were tears running down her cheeks. I skidded to a halt when I saw her face. Jessica was right, this was big for Mom.

We stood staring at each other for a moment and then both spoke at the exact same time, "Are you okay?"

Mom made an indecipherable sound and reached out to yank me in for a hug. And I hugged back. Hard.

"I'd like to meet him, officially," I whispered into her shoulder.

"Okay, sweetie," she whispered back.

All my discomfort melted away in her hug, but was back as soon as we pulled apart and I looked into her eyes.

"Are you scared, Mom?" I asked quietly.

"Yes. Are you?"

"Yeah, but I don't know why. Maybe nervous is a better word." I looked at the dirt. "Jessica thinks you might be scared about…" I sighed. I couldn't talk about this. It was too big for me. I lifted my gaze from the dirt and glanced at her face. She had stopped crying and was studying me intently.

"What?" I asked.

Mom stepped into the grass at the side of the road and beckoned to me to follow. We found a place to sit and while she stared off into the distance, I pulled blades of grass and chewed them into oblivion.

"There are so many things coming up for me that I haven't thought about in years. And other things that I think about almost every day. But you don't need to worry about me, Cedar. That's not your job." She touched my hair.

"Well, whose job is it then? I thought we were a team. Family worries about each other, right?"

She grabbed me again and squished me into her. When she finally let go of me, I repositioned my glasses while she blew her nose on her hankie.

"You're such a good boy. And I think we need to go home and talk with the rest of the team."

"The Grands?" I asked.

"They can worry about me, I can worry about you. Okay?"

"Okay," I said.

We decided to take Jessica home, regroup – Mom's word – and make a plan for coming back to see Shell together the following day.

When we got to Jessica's house, I got her stuff out of the trunk and followed her as she clumped up the cracked sidewalk to the front door. She stopped there and turned to face me. "Just leave my stuff here. I'll get one of the animals to bring it in." She tossed her head in the direction of the house. I could hear several voices shouting and laughing. Saturday mornings at Jess's tended to be even more chaotic than most mornings, usually with extra friends over to amplify the noise.

Jessica turned around carefully on her crutches and faced me. She cleared her throat.

"Listen, Charles," she said. "I know I always have something to say about everything, but I don't have a clue what to say this time. This is big. I'm trying to imagine how this must feel for you and I really can't. Or for your mom. So, I guess…"

I shuffled my feet uncomfortably. How many heart-to-heart talks could one guy handle in a day?

She grabbed my shoulders and gave me that little shake she does. "I just want you to know that you can talk to me. And I promise to do my very best to just listen and not talk. Too much. Okay?" Then, for the first time since grade two (when I chipped a tooth on the monkey bars), Jessica hugged me. "Okay?" she said again.

"Okay," I whispered. "Thanks."

Then we went to the Grands'. I thought we were just going to ask if we could keep the car for another day, but I was sent to the store for a bunch of things no one really needed. When I got back, all three of them were sitting at the kitchen table looking uncomfortable.

"Have a seat, honey," Mom said.

Grandpa was frowning and drumming his fingers and Grandma was fidgeting with the buttons on her sweater.

Mom was playing with her hair. Not a good sign. "What?" I said.

"Well, there's one more thing you need to know before we go visit your father tomorrow." She looked at Grandma and Grandpa.

This was getting weird. "Okay. What is it?"

"Well, you know how I told you that Shell never knew I was pregnant? Well, that wasn't true."

The only sound was Grandma's fingernails clicking against her big brown buttons.

"He knew? How did he know?" I asked.

"I did have his address and I wrote him and told him I was pregnant."

"And you told him not to contact you?" I asked quietly, hope draining out of me.

"No," she said softly. "I told him how to reach me and left it up to him if he wanted to be involved."

"And?"

"He sent me a cheque for $500 and wished me well."

Even the button-clicking stopped.

"Anything else?" I was staring at my hands and could barely get my voice all the way to the table.

"That's it, Cedar. I'm sorry, honey. And I'm sorry I lied, but when I never heard from him again, I thought the story I told you would be … easier for you."

And in that instant, everything changed.

I wasn't a boy whose father didn't know about him; I was a boy whose father didn't want him. I pushed back my chair and stood up.

"I … can I …"

Grandpa cleared his throat. "You can use my study."

I locked the door behind me and plopped down

into Grandpa's big leather office chair. I couldn't slow my thoughts down enough to deal with them one at a time. Shell knew he had a kid. Had he guessed who I was when he was looking at me?

I got up and paced back and forth the few steps it took to cross the study. I returned to Grandpa's chair. Up again. More pacing.

The facts started rearranging themselves so they wouldn't hurt so much: maybe Shell had a good reason for staying out of my life, maybe he was a secret agent and he was protecting us by keeping our identities secret. If anyone knew he had family...

I made myself stop. Good grief, my imagination!

What about Mom? She had lied. I don't think it had ever occurred to me before that my mom could lie to me. *Would* lie to me. And if that was possible, how did I know she wasn't lying now? Maybe she was just saying this to keep me away from him. That thought brought a wave of feelings I couldn't identify, but none of them felt good. I needed to go back to the kitchen and ask some more questions.

When I grabbed the knob, I heard a weird sound and stopped. I pressed my ear against the door and listened.

Mom was crying. It didn't sound like someone in the middle of a lie or a scheme. It was the saddest sound I'd ever heard and I knew she was telling the truth about Shell.

I can't explain how, but suddenly, I was able to see the situation through my mom's eyes. I got abandoned by someone who didn't know me, she got abandoned by someone who did know her.

I went back to the kitchen table and sat down.

"I don't want to go tomorrow," I said quietly.

My mom was blowing her nose and wiping her eyes, so my grandpa answered.

"No problem, Charles. You take your time. You can always track him down again when you're older."

"Or not," I said.

"Or not," he agreed.

I looked at my mom's crazy hippie hair and red-rimmed eyes.

"I know you and I are different, but I think you're brave and strong. You're a good mom."

Shocked silence.

Grandpa clapped me on the back so hard he almost loosened a tooth. "Good man!" he bellowed in his trying-not-to-cry voice.

"Oh, Charles," said my mom.

I blushed. "It's okay, Mom – you can call me Cedar."

So, a year has gone by and when I think about last summer's adventure, it seems like a single point in time rather than the most action-packed week of my life. Like a field of fresh snow got rolled into a giant ball and then packed down into one little snowball: *How I met my father.*

Going back to school after camp was the worst. Trying to avoid talking about why I got sent home was brutal. Good old Jessica saved me on more than one occasion, telling people to mind their own beeswax, with a reinforcing snarl when necessary. The only good part was that the camp Talent Night ended up being a fiasco so most people were more interested in talking about that than my expulsion. After Dylan and I were sent home, our Talent Night group had tried to throw something different together for the show at the last minute. I never got all the details, but keywords include: *Kevin, sugar,* and *fire.* I'll let you fill in the blanks.

I know you are dying to know so here you go: yes, I did get my hair cut.

Mom was weird for a while after camp. Grandma was too. I definitely was. Grandpa is always Grandpa.

Anyhow, one morning a couple of weeks after I got home, Mom and I were eating porridge and I was thinking how nice it would be to have a bowl of sugar-infested, store-bought cereal or even some tomato soup-flavoured pancakes, when Mom asked how I was enjoying my porridge. I was about to lie and tell her it was good, when it hit me that I couldn't keep pretending I liked porridge because I didn't want to hurt her feelings. After all, I'd been griping about porridge for years before I met my father. It was time for us to stop tiptoeing around each other.

"I hate porridge and I always have," I said quietly. "I'm sorry if that hurts your feelings, but I hate it!"

She looked at me for a while with an unreadable expression on her face. I decided I might as well go for it.

"And I'm getting a haircut."

"That's probably a good idea, sweetie," she said. "You could get Grandpa to take you to his barber."

"Grandpa has a barber? He has, like, twelve hairs."

She laughed. "You'll look great with short hair."

I frowned at her. "Why are you changing your mind?" I asked suspiciously.

She shrugged. "Time to move on. One way or the other. Time to let go."

"Mom, if I hadn't come along, would you be living in a tree?"

She looked at me for a second, then burst out laughing. "I really don't think so, but you never know. I feel as strongly about how we are trashing our world as I did back then, but I see other ways of trying to make a difference. Why do you ask?"

I shrugged. "No reason. Just thinking about all those people willing to live in tents, to give up everything really, to try to save some trees. Obviously, it's more important than I thought. I might come with you to that climate change rally next week."

She started glowing and tearing up, so I escaped to my room.

But I thought about Mom's "moving on" comment for a long time. Long after my hair was cut (and it looked good).

I thought about it as I started my new school, which was one of the hardest things ever. Jessica was right about needing a break from the same little group of kids and now I feel that breath of fresh air she was talking about, but the first week of school nearly killed me.

I'd gotten pretty used to relying on Jessica for all those moments when I didn't really know what to do with myself. My first week at Jefferson, every moment that I wasn't in class I was adrift – a boat with no oars. I didn't know what to do at break. I hid in a bathroom stall. I pretended to search for lost things in my locker. I even bought a fake phone at the dollar store to pretend I was texting at lunch hour. It was horrible. I felt anxious to the point of nausea all the time.

The weekend after my first week at Jefferson, I called Jessica and confessed how bad it was and she said, "Chuck, get yourself involved. Clubs, dude! Is there a chess club?"

"Won't that make it worse? Signing up for the Geek Club? I can already tell you what the cool kids will do with that."

"Since when do you care about that crap? You've been best friends with a girl your whole life, you big loser! And I have grown up under the dark shadow of boy cooties! But we survived because we had each other. Join stuff. Jefferson is a big school. Your people are there somewhere."

By the time we got together for her first math tutorial after the third week of school, I had met two guys (yes – through chess club) named Justin and Darth. Well, Darth is not his real name, but he won't even tell anyone what it is. Obviously, he is obsessed with Star Wars. It's actually a better series than I thought. Even the old movies are pretty good.

Anyway, Jessica and her new friends always invite me and the guys to meet them for pizza at a place about halfway between our two schools and we always laugh our butts off. I think Darth might have a thing for Jessica's friend Naomi.

Jessica and I have both moved on and we are having new and different experiences, but we're still best friends. My life has changed in many ways, but we're getting older and that's life. We're always moving on, aren't we?

My final news is that I got a postcard from Shell a few weeks ago. Turns out my mom had called Camp Mingle and asked someone to take a message over to Shell. She gave him our address, but not our phone number. Told him the true identity of Scrawny Kid, Superhero. I didn't know anything about it until I got the postcard. I had decided months ago that I wasn't interested in having a dad after all. Not that dad, anyway. He made his choice thirteen years ago.

But I liked getting the postcard.

Oh, I almost forgot. Mom has a boyfriend now. Kurt. He was the boss at one of the offices where she worked. He caught her snooping around in the files one day and she told him she was *looking for the real environmental policies, Mr. Man!* Apparently, it was love at first sight. And his company is truly green. *Thank the goddess,* said my crazy hippie mother.

I might get in touch with Shell one day. Maybe when I'm older. When I'm sure I won't get him confused with my fantasy dad – because let's face it, who could compete with the Superman/Santa combo?

Now that I think about it, Grandma is Santa in a saggy sweater. And Mom is practically Superman; she may even save the planet one day. And Grandpa has been an awesome father. A grand one.

Well, I guess that's everything.

I have to go get ready. It's Boys' Night Out. Grandpa is taking me out for steaks and then to see *Zombie Transformers.* Mom thinks we're going for tofu curry and a documentary.

Don't tell her!

GRATITUDE

Whew! We did it! A heartfelt thank you to all my readers for your time and thoughtful feedback, to my wonderful community of cheerleaders, and to the excellent team at Yellow Dog.

Thank you, Dave Jenkinson, for sharing your time and expertise with such generosity and good humour.